The
Princess School

Princess Charming

The
Princess School

If the Shoe Fits

Who's the Fairest?

Let Down Your Hair

Beauty Is a Beast

Princess Charming

The Princess School

Princess Charming

Jane B. Mason ✌ Sarah Hines Stephens

SCHOLASTIC INC.

New York Toronto London Auckland Sydney
Mexico City New Delhi Hong Kong Buenos Aires

Copyright © 2005 by Jane B. Mason and Sarah Hines Stephens.

All rights reserved.
Published by Scholastic Inc.
SCHOLASTIC and associated logos are trademarks
and/or registered trademarks of Scholastic Inc.

ISBN 0-439-69813-8

12 11 10 9 8 7 6 5 4 3 2 1   5 6 7 8 9 10/0

Printed in the U.S.A.   40

First printing, May 2005

For our own Queen Mothers, who rule.

—JBM & SHS

The
Princess School

Princess Charming

Chapter One

A Harsh Blow

"Ooof!" Prince Valerian tumbled off his steed and hit the lawn in front of his castle with a dull thud.

"Oh, sorry." Rapunzel Arugula, who had unseated the prince, swung down from her own steed and offered the prince a hand. "I didn't mean to hit you that hard," she said. She shouldered her practice lance with a natural grace.

Refusing Rapunzel's help, Val got to his feet and rubbed his shoulder. "It wasn't that hard," he insisted with a wince. "Doesn't hurt."

Rapunzel raised her eyebrows at Cinderella Brown, Briar Rose, and William Dapper. The three of them sat in the shade of a lemon tree watching Rapunzel and Val's jousting practice. Rose hid her smile demurely behind her hand, but Dap laughed out loud.

Rapunzel felt a little bit bad. The blow may not have been that hard, but she had hit Val in the same spot (and unseated him) at least twenty times that morning. She knew it had to hurt. And not just his shoulder, either. Val was a talented jouster and known for his sense of pride.

"You're going to have to move more quickly during the competition," Dap told Val with a grin. "It's a good thing Rapunzel isn't enrolled at Charm School. If she was, you might not be the tournament favorite."

Rapunzel smiled. There was a time when she had wished more than anything that she could go to The Charm School for Boys, where Val and Dap were second-year students. But that was before she started having so much fun at Princess School — back before she'd made friends with Ella, Snow, and Rose, three other first-year Bloomers.

Rapunzel pushed her homemade steed back to the starting position at the top of the rail slope. She patted the barrel's mop head, and prepared to ease into the saddle for another run. Though she held her tongue, she couldn't hide her smile. Dap was right. Val was indeed the best jouster in his class — the favorite to take the heats in his year and have a chance at the Charm School jousting tournament title. But Rapunzel was the one training him. And doing a fantastic job of it, too.

"How about one more run?" Rapunzel challenged Val. He stooped to retrieve his shield, and when he straightened he seemed to have regained his energy.

Rapunzel had to hand it to him. The proud prince was always up for a challenge, even after hours of being knocked off his horse. And with the annual tournament just over a week away, he knew he needed all the practice he could get . . . even if he wouldn't admit it.

Val sprang back onto his mount. "En garde!" he shouted.

"This time, I want you to try to hit my shield in the center, and low," Rapunzel coached. "Aim for the bottom of the crest." Their shields and lances were really just boards and broomsticks. But the balance and the blows were the same. Val had wanted to practice with real horses, shields, and weapons. But his father had told him they would only be damaged. "Next year," he'd said. "You're still a bit green yet."

Of course Val had bristled at that. Secretly Rapunzel thought it had given him an edge — a desire to push himself even harder. Not that the tournament prize wasn't motivation enough. The winner would be granted full access to the Farthingdale Stables, the most stupendous stables in all the land. They housed dozens of well-trained quarter horses, Morgans, and Arabians. They were surrounded by training circuits and woodland paths. The winner's entire class would be given a tour, learn about horse care, and be allowed to ride the noble beasts. Rapunzel knew that Val had the desire both for the prize and to prove himself to his father. She also knew firsthand how much he'd improved with practice. Val would be a fierce competitor.

Holding her shield — not too tightly — against her shoulder, Rapunzel kicked her "horse" into action and rolled toward Val. Val did as he had been told and dealt Rapunzel a sturdy blow to the lower middle part of her shield with his lance. Had she been holding too tightly, she would have been unseated. As it was she had to check her balance.

"Good one!" she cheered the prince.

"I hope I didn't hit you too hard," Val said. He did not hide the pride in his voice.

"You don't see me on the ground, do you?" Rapunzel retorted. "But I think that blow would be enough to unseat a prince." She turned to her audience. "And speaking of princes, Dap, would you like to try your hand?" she asked.

"Against you? Not on your life!" Dap scooted closer toward the trunk of the lemon tree, and Ella and Rose laughed.

"How about against 'the favorite' then? You *are* planning to compete, are you not?" Rapunzel asked.

Dap shrugged. "Every prince in the school is competing. So I suppose I am, too." He stood and stretched his lanky arms and legs before taking the broomstick and shield from Rapunzel and pushing the "horse" back up the track. "I guess I can give our Val a go." He swung one of his long legs up and over the saddle, almost knocking the mop head of his steed off with his own.

On the other side of the lawn, Val shook his head. "I apologize in advance, my friend," he said brashly.

Rapunzel sat down with Ella and Rose to watch.

"Where's Snow?" Rapunzel asked, suddenly realizing their fair-skinned friend was missing.

"Late," Rose said with a shrug. "But I'm sure she'll be here soon."

"Is Val really the tournament favorite?" Ella asked.

"I thought the Charming boys always won," Rose added.

"They usually do." Rapunzel nodded. "Lars Charming won the last two years. He was the youngest ever to win the title. He took it from the oldest Charming as a second-year. There are rumors Hans could unseat his brother this year. And there's a new fourth-year, Emmett Pantaloon, who has quite a bit of jousting talent. But Val has a really good chance if —" she looked over at Val, who sat ridiculously straight in his saddle and eyed Dap as if they were archenemies — "if he can get over himself," she finished.

"So Dap is no threat?" Rose asked.

"Only to himself," Ella giggled. Dap had managed

to get his leg caught up in the stirrup. He was looking down and rolling forward, right toward Val's broomstick.

Rapunzel cringed as the princes came together with a *thunk* and a *thud*. In a split second Dap was on the ground with his shield over his face and his foot still hung up in the stirrup. Fortunately his legs were so long that his torso rested safely on the grass.

Ella and Rose leaped to their feet to help Dap out of his bind. Val slipped off his horse and paraded around like a peacock, holding his practice lance high. "I can take any prince, anytime, anywhere!" he boasted, puffing out his chest.

Rapunzel smirked and exchanged a knowing glance with Ella.

"How about any princ-*ess*?" Rose asked slyly. "I have not seen you unseat your instructor today. And by the by, aren't all of those fancy moves tricks that you learned from *her*?"

"Of course I haven't knocked Rapunzel off," Val said, looking surprised and horrified at the same time. "But that does not make her the better jouster. It simply makes me the better prince."

Rapunzel's jaw dropped open. "Are you telling me you have been taking it easy on me? That you haven't been riding your best?" She stared straight at Val, eye to eye. "Have I been wasting my time training with you all month?" Rapunzel planted her hands on her hips and waited for an answer.

Ella, Dap, and Rose looked from Rapunzel to Val and back. Val gulped.

"Your moves are great," Val said. "I really appreciate you training with me. It's not that. It's just that I have to let you win because, well, you're a princess. Don't take it personally. Besides, any Charm School boy could beat a Princess School girl."

Three pairs of princess eyes bored into Val. The foundering prince looked to Dap for some support. "Right?"

Dap put up his hands and backed away. He wanted no part in the conversation.

Rapunzel let a big breath out her nose. If she'd been a dragon she would have been breathing flames. She was used to Val's boasting and teasing — but this was different. This was serious. "I could take on any boy at Charm School and beat him in a fair fight," she said evenly. "It has *nothing* to do with being a princess, and *everything* to do with being a superior jouster."

Val took a step backward. "Look, even if you were the best jouster in the land, we would never know," he said seriously. "There is not a prince in the kingdom who would truly take arms against a princess."

Grinding her teeth, Rapunzel searched for something else to say. Her hands were balled into fists. She wanted to leap on the barrel-back pony and plow Val down with such force it would take him several minutes to get up. But deep, deep down she knew he was right.

The chivalry code all of the boys at Charm followed forbade them to take arms against a girl. In fact, it had taken quite a bit of convincing just to get Val to let Rapunzel train with him. Convincing, and skill. He'd insisted it was inappropriate. Then Rapunzel reminded him how often they had played at jousting with branches in the woods when she would escape from her tower. And how great her lance skills were. When jousting began at Charm School, Val suddenly wanted desperately to learn Rapunzel's innovative moves. He knew he would need every ounce of finesse he could absorb to beat the brawn of the bigger boys at Charm. Couldn't he see he would need it to beat her fairly, too?

Before Rapunzel could find her tongue to give Val the lashing he deserved, a soft voice called everyone's attention.

"Yoo-hoo! Sorry I'm late!" A dark-haired figure crested the hill. She was waving, and so red in the face Rapunzel almost didn't recognize her.

Snow White stood before them, panting. "Am I late?" she asked with a sweet smile. "I hope I haven't missed anything!"

Chapter Two
Fair Fight

"Those pompous princes!" Rapunzel fumed. "The whole pack of them can go . . . go . . ." She was so angry she couldn't even think of a terrible enough place to send them. "And they can take their stupid chivalry with them!" she shouted.

Rapunzel stormed down the path away from Val's castle so fast that Ella, Snow, and Rose almost had to run to keep up with her. "I can accept that some of the princes might be better jousters than I am. But I cannot accept that they will not battle me fair and square." Her eyes began to feel moist, which made her even angrier. "How will I ever know how good I am if I don't have a chance to fight?"

"Why won't they fight you?" Snow asked, still breathing heavily. "Are they afraid?"

"Probably." Rapunzel couldn't help but smile.

"Certainly!" Rose nodded.

"But it's more than that," Rapunzel explained as

they neared the rickety wooden bridge that crossed Troll Creek. "It's because of this hair, and this dress, and everything about me. It's because I'm a girl."

"But surely you can change out of your dress," Snow said. Her big dark eyes were filled with confusion.

Rapunzel turned to her friend.

Poor Snow was still pink-cheeked and confused. She'd missed more than the practice this morning, she'd missed a battle! She deserved a little explanation. Then again, so did Rapunzel.

"What kept you this morning?" Rapunzel asked as she stepped onto the creaking bridge. Suddenly a deep raspy voice sang out from below her:

Crossing my creek?
You'd best have loot!
To use my bridge
You must have fruit!

"He did." Snow looked nervously at the yellow eyes staring up between the bridge slats.

Rapunzel nodded. The bridge troll was a real pain.

"I forgot my fruit. Sort of. It's a long story," Snow sighed. "But I couldn't cross the bridge. I had to run down to the lane crossing. And I don't have even a berry to get back across!"

"Don't worry." Rapunzel dug into the enormous pockets she had fashioned into her skirts, pulled out four lemons she had picked from Val's tree, and tossed

10

the fruit to the bridge troll. The troll reached up from under the bridge and caught three lemons in his rough brown hands. The fourth he caught in his mouth.

A moment later the troll spat out a mouthful of yellow pulp and bitter peel. "Lemons!" he snarled. "I ought to make you swim."

"The cost to cross is one piece of fruit," Rapunzel replied with a shrug. "You never specified which kind. Besides, sour should be just right for you." She pushed her way past the grimacing troll and motioned to her friends to follow.

The troll was annoying, but Rapunzel knew he wasn't really dangerous. Besides, she was much more annoyed with Val. "You know what, Snow?" Rapunzel said, stomping down the path. "I *am* going to change out of my dress!"

"Into what?" Ella looked at Rapunzel like she had lost her mind.

"Into breeches and a suit of armor!" Rapunzel said, leaping onto a large tree stump. "If I can't compete as a princess I will do it as a prince. I am going to trick that pack of fancy lads into jousting with me as an equal. I'll beat them all at their own tournament and show Val I really am the best jouster in the land."

"Rapunzel in shining armor . . . it'll be just like the masquerade," Rose said. A smile grew on her face as Rapunzel jumped off her stump.

"Only this time I have to make sure that *nobody* is able to guess who I am," Rapunzel said seriously. "I'm going to need all of you to help."

Ella was still looking at Rapunzel like she was crazy and Snow was waving to three billy goats approaching the bridge, but Rose's enthusiasm was building.

"It's a great idea!" Rose crowed. "I wish I had thought of it myself — not that I am a good jouster. I mean I might be, I've never tried, but . . . you know what I mean. It's perfect. And perfect for you, Rapunzel."

"Well, after I win I can teach you," Rapunzel said. "The prize is full access to Farthingdale Stables," she added, grabbing Snow's attention.

"All of those hoofed beauties." Snow cupped her hands near her face as if she were nuzzling a horse's muzzle. "I *would* love to meet them." She sighed.

"It sounds a little dangerous," Ella said quietly. Rapunzel and Rose nodded and grinned, obviously excited about the scheme. "Are you sure this is what you want?" Ella asked, putting her hand on Rapunzel's shoulder.

"A chance to prove myself to those Charmless boys and Val? You bet," Rapunzel said.

"What if you get hurt . . . or caught?" Ella asked.

"Yes, what if you get caught?" Snow echoed.

Rapunzel waved Ella's fears aside with her hand. "By the time they find out who I am I'll already have

12

won. They'll never know what struck them. And not one of them will strike me. I promise."

"You can train with one of my father's horses," Rose offered. "Barrels and mop heads won't do for our champion." She clapped Rapunzel on the back. "And I'm sure I can come up with some armor, too."

"Perfect. I won't be able to borrow Val's like I did for the masquerade. I want to make sure he is the most surprised of all. I still can't believe he said those things. He's supposed to be my friend!" Rapunzel's scowl started to sneak its way back onto her face.

"Well, if you are going to do this right, just any old breeches won't do. You'll need a Charm School uniform," Ella said a little grudgingly. "I can stitch one for you."

"You can?" Rapunzel's grin returned full force and she caught Ella in a barreling hug. "Thanks, Ella!"

Snow looked at Rapunzel with admiration. "Golly, I can't believe you're really going to do this!" she said.

"I'll have to get busy on some new moves. I taught Val everything he knows, and unfortunately everything I know, too." She drummed her fingers on her chin. Since Val knew her best stuff, she would simply have to come up with something even better. New moves would be key. "Those lads in Charm School are so hung up on tradition. A bit of innovation will unseat them for sure!"

Chapter Three

Hill of Beans

Waving good-bye to her friends, Snow skipped down the woodland path toward the dwarves' cottage. She hummed a little tune and her mind drifted. Rapunzel's plan to joust at the Charm School tournament was exciting, and nobody would enjoy meeting the horses at Farthingdale more than Snow would. But for some reason all she could think about were the three beans in her pocket.

Snow ran her fingers over the small, smooth beans. They felt like soft pebbles . . . and something more, though she wasn't sure what.

Snow stopped in the trail as she approached the spot where she had gotten the beans just a little while before. This was definitely the place. The grass was still flat where the boy who had traded her the beans had been sitting by the side of the path, crying. And look, there next to the spot was an apple core.

Snow hadn't started down the path intending to trade her bag of apples for the three beans. In fact, she almost hadn't noticed the boy as she hurried along, hoping to arrive on time for Rapunzel and Val's jousting practice. It was his sniffling that had made her stop.

"Are you hurt?" Snow had asked, stopping in alarm.

"No," the boy had wailed. "I've been tricked." As soon as he had said it he started to bawl harder than ever.

Snow had put down her bag of apples. She simply had to comfort the poor fellow. What else could she do?

"Talk it out. Scream and shout. Tell me what it's all about." She had recited one of the dwarves' wise poems. "Maybe you will feel better if you tell me about it," she said more plainly.

And so he had. "My mother is going to be so angry." He snuffled. "She sent me to the market to sell our old cow Henrietta, but on the way I met a stranger. She seemed nice and she wanted to make a trade." Then the boy had unleashed a fresh batch of tears. Just remembering it made Snow feel a little teary herself.

"I didn't really want to walk all the way to the market with our stubborn cow," the boy had continued after mopping his face with Snow's lace handkerchief.

"But I don't know what made me agree to such a bad trade. That lady must have been a witch!"

"It can't be that bad," Snow had said, giving the boy's arm a little pat.

"Just look," he'd answered, opening his fist. "I traded our cow for three measly beans!"

Snow had nearly gasped when she saw the beans. A whole cow for them *did* seem like a bad trade. She had felt awful for the boy. She knew all about dealing with witches — and angry mothers, too, for that matter.

"I think they look like fine beans!" Snow had said, trying to sound chipper. "Why, I would give my whole bag of apples for three beans as nice as those!"

"You would?" For the first time Snow saw the boy perk up.

"Sure!" she'd answered. It had taken her most of the morning to pick the apples, which she'd planned to give to the grumpy bridge troll. Even though it cost just one piece of fruit per crossing, Snow had figured the testy little troll could use some extra sweetness. Snow realized with a start that if she traded her apples for the boy's beans, she would have nothing to offer the bridge troll and he wouldn't let her cross. *But I told the boy I would do it*, she'd thought. Snow White was always true to her word.

Snow had handed over the sack of apples and quick

as a wink, the boy's tears had dried. He'd pulled out an apple and started eating it on the spot. "Delicious," he'd said with his mouth full. Juice dribbled down his chin. Then he'd shouldered the big bag of apples and started off without even a thank-you.

"What's your name?" Snow had called after him as he tossed the core away.

"Jack," he'd yelled. "Here, don't forget your beans!" And he threw the beans lightheartedly in the air, making Snow scramble to pick them out of the dirt.

"It was worth it," Snow said to herself now, continuing down the path toward home. "Even if the beans don't grow, at least I made that poor boy much happier. Gosh, I hope his mother liked the apples."

It had been worth missing jousting practice. During her run down to the lane crossing, Snow had grown more and more excited about the beans. It had been all she could do to keep them a secret from her friends. She wanted to wait and show them when she had bean plants growing in her garden.

As the dwarves' neat little cottage came into view, Snow hurried to collect her spade and watering can from the shed. Then, with a breeze catching her skirt, she scurried around to the garden plot in the back.

Snow dug three small holes in the dark, rich dirt and dropped a bean in each one. Then she made a mound over them, tucking them carefully into their cozy beds before giving them a drink.

"There," she said, patting the soil. "Grow well, little beans." With a smile Snow ducked back around the cottage to put her tools away. All she had to do now was wait and see what came up.

Chapter Four

Feeling Sore

Rapunzel led Triumph, Rose's father's horse, back into Rose's family stables and gave him a pat on the nose before handing him over to the stable hand.

"Thanks, Triumph," she said. "And thanks to you, too, Rose. You really didn't have to get up this early." The sun was just starting to peek over the horizon, and Rapunzel and Rose had already been up for over an hour.

"You said it was important, and now that I've seen your new moves I believe it!" Rose said excitedly. She was leading her own favorite horse, Victory. "Your twisting thrust and sideways tuck are going to bowl those princes right over!"

Rapunzel did not want to be a braggart like Val, but she had to agree. She had come up with the moves late at night in her tower, galloping around in circles and picturing the joust course in her head. She'd thought the moves would be good, but she hadn't known for sure until she tried them out today. Rapunzel had knocked her opponent out every time. And even though her opponent was just a scarecrow, thanks to Rose she had been able to practice on a real *horse* and with a real lance, too!

Next to Rapunzel, Rose struggled to take the scarecrow's limp body off of Victory's saddle. "A hand would be nice," she said, straining under the weight.

Rapunzel blinked. "Sorry," she said, reaching up to help. Together she and Rose carried the stuffed knight into a stall and propped it up on a bale of hay.

"You'd better rest up." Rose wagged her finger at the flopping prince. "She's going to be back this afternoon for another round!"

"I hope he can take it." Rapunzel laughed. Though they had given the prince a crown of flowers, he was not looking very well. His straw stuffing was spilling out of at least three holes and his pumpkin head was askew. "I'm a little worried about him," she admitted.

"I don't think he's the one you have to worry about," Rose said, ushering Rapunzel out of the barn.

Rapunzel knew exactly what Rose meant. She was talking about Val. "You're right. We'd better hurry — if I am late to our meeting spot he'll continue on to the tower and discover that I'm not home. That might make him suspicious!"

"Exactly," Rose said.

Rapunzel ran down the path after Rose, even though being late was not exactly what she was worried about. Or at least not exactly *everything* she was worried about. She and Val hadn't talked since their last practice, not since their fight the day before. Rapunzel was thrilled about her plan to compete in the joust — but keeping a secret from Val felt strange and uncomfortable.

"Halloo!" Val called as the girls approached the giant oak where Val and Rapunzel met each morning for the walk to school.

"Halloo to you, too," Rose called back.

If Val was surprised to see Rose with Rapunzel, he didn't show it. He and Rapunzel usually walked to school alone. But Val was not a prince to question a little extra time in the company of Briar Rose, and — Rapunzel noted with relief — he was too excited about other things to ask questions.

"You won't believe what has happened," Val said as soon as the girls were closer than shouting distance. "Mother and Father got me a new lance — a real one!"

Rapunzel smiled. She knew Val had been yearning for a real lance for ages. She also was glad to see he wasn't still sore about their quarrel. But then she felt a twinge of anger that Val had brushed off their fight so easily. It just seemed to prove that he hadn't been taking Rapunzel seriously. *Well, he'll have to take me seriously soon*, she thought. He might have gotten over it, but Rapunzel had not forgotten a single heated word of their last conversation. Val's indifference to their fight only made her extra determined to win the Charm School tournament. Setting her jaw, she walked briskly down the path toward school with Val and Rose trailing behind her.

"I can't wait to try it out," Val babbled on, too pleased with his new lance to notice the shift in Rapunzel's mood. "I have the shields ready, and I am almost certain my parents will let us use the horses this afternoon. You'll come, won't you?" He looked imploringly at Rapunzel. "And you, too, of course," he added for Rose's benefit.

Rapunzel grimaced. Val did love an audience.

"This afternoon? I can't." Rapunzel searched for an excuse. "I'll be busy, um —"

"Helping me with a new 'do for Looking Glass," Rose blurted.

Val flashed Rapunzel a sly grin. "Surely you jest!"

Rapunzel was certain he didn't believe it. Val knew her better than to think she would choose primping over a good gallop with a weapon. But it was too late now.

"I'm afraid not. It's really a rather important and challenging new braid we have to master," Rapunzel said, trying to sound convincing. "Madame Spiegel will be quizzing us on it tomorrow in class."

"But I need you," Val said, his face going from amused to hurt. "I mean, I know I can take the first-years without even trying, and my class isn't much of a challenge. But Hans told me he and Lars got new lances, too. And they have been getting pointers from their uncle, Sir Charisma, as well. I have to prepare as much as I possibly can!"

The panic in Val's voice was hard to take. Rapunzel had heard of Sir Charisma. He was the undefeated jousting champion of Afaraway Land for several years running. Rapunzel felt torn. She wanted to help Val but she needed to help herself first. Didn't she?

"Is that the trumpet?" Rose grabbed Rapunzel's arm and waved good-bye to Val as she pulled her friend across the bridge over the swan-filled moat surrounding the Princess School castle.

Rapunzel hadn't heard a thing, but she picked up her skirts and ran the rest of the way to hearthroom by Rose's side, grateful for the exit. As angry as she was about Val's ridiculous declarations, she was quickly discovering that she did not like keeping secrets from him. After all, they had been sharing secrets for years! It was hard to break the habit. As she and Rose sped noiselessly down the marble corridor, Rapunzel felt terribly torn.

"You've worked with him enough," Rose said. "Besides, doesn't he get to practice all day while we sit in class?"

Stepping into the regal hearthroom chamber, Rapunzel realized Rose was right. She had done plenty for Val. She was the one who needed practice! The kings and queens portrayed in the tapestries on the stone walls looked on with fixed expressions. They seemed in perfect agreement.

Ella beamed when she saw Rose and Rapunzel, and hurried over to them. "I found Hag's and Prune's old cloaks in the basement. They're the same colors as the Charm School uniforms — purple and green! I would have gotten started in earnest, but Kastrid decided it was time for an 'airing-out.' I had to hang out all of the rugs and tapestries and beat the dust out of them." Ella rolled her eyes. "It's just as well, since I should probably do some measuring first. Are we meeting in the stables again at lunch?"

Rapunzel nodded but winced as she slid into her ornately carved high-back chair beside Rose. She hated the thought of adding one more chore to Ella's impossibly long list. And she was wincing for another reason. After galloping on Triumph all morning she was sore. Riding a real horse felt quite different from riding a barrel. Rapunzel prided herself on being far from delicate, but today she could have used twenty cushions.

"Thank you so much, Ella." Rapunzel managed a smile. "I don't know how I would do this without you." She wished she could confide that she was getting nervous about how she was going to do it at all. Certainly she had the skill. Surely her new moves were surprising enough. But the boys at Charm had loads more training and practice time. Rapunzel kept smiling even though it felt false. She didn't want to bog down her friends with her worries. And just then the final trumpet sounded and Madame Garabaldi swept into the room.

As the instructor paced the front of the chamber, reading from a long scroll of announcements, Rapunzel strained to hear the sounds of the Charm School boys starting their day across the garden. At first she was not sure if the distant *thumps* were the sound of hoofs falling. But a moment later the unmistakable clash of metal and cry of "Hold!" echoed in the air.

Rapunzel scowled. Rose was right. Val didn't need her to practice. He was allowed to joust all day while she sat here under the watchful —

Suddenly, Rapunzel's eyes went wide. She twisted in her seat. She could not believe she had not thought of this before!

The Charm School jousting tournament, just like their jousting practice, was going to take place while Rapunzel was supposed to be at Princess School. She had to find a way to get out of class — a lot of class!

Rapunzel fidgeted. She wished she could interrupt Madame Garabaldi to tell her friends her dilemma right that minute. The impervious instructor seemed to read Rapunzel's mind and stopped to look up from her scroll. She stared at Rapunzel for a long moment.

"Do stop shifting so in your seat, Rapunzel," she reprimanded. "You look as if you are waiting to race out of here. Very unbecoming."

With a gulp and an apologetic smile, Rapunzel straightened up and sat still.

Ella and Rose looked at her sympathetically, but Snow did not look up at all. And she hadn't come over to say hello before trumpet, either, Rapunzel suddenly realized.

That's odd, Rapunzel thought, breathing deeply to ease the pain in her bottom.

She'd have to find out what was going on with Snow later. Right now another question burned in Rapunzel's mind. How in the world was she going to escape the eagle eye of Madame Garabaldi and her other instructors in order to compete in the joust?

Chapter Five
Minor Complications

Ella slumped against a bale of hay and rubbed her eyes. She was so tired she could barely see straight, but she tried her best to do just that. Before her, Rapunzel was proudly modeling the Charm School uniform that Ella had finished sewing as the horizon grew light that very morning. It fit perfectly, and Rapunzel was practically jumping up and down.

"I love it, I love it, I love it!" she shouted.

Ella stifled a yawn and smiled up at her friend. The four girls had been meeting in the stables every day that week to strategize and to practice, but today Rapunzel seemed even more excited than usual. Ella felt pleased that the uniform had turned out so well. And when she saw the look of pure happiness on Rapunzel's face, she knew that staying up until dawn and burning all her candle stubs was worth it.

"Try it with the armor," Rose said, holding up a

long-sleeved tunic made of thick fabric and interlocking metal rings. "The arming doublet comes first."

Rapunzel slipped it on, and she and Rose tied the lacings in the front. Then Rose readied several metal leg pieces for Rapunzel to step into — one for her foot, one for her calf, one for her knee, and yet another for her thigh. There were several pieces for her arms, plus a backplate and breastplate to cover her torso. Rose deftly fastened buckles and inserted pins in hinges.

"You'd make a wonderful squire, Rose," Rapunzel said with a grin.

"My parents used to make me wear protective armor around the house!" Rose giggled. "They're always so scared I'm going to injure myself on a soupspoon or a sewing needle. I had to take a course in the proper placement and names of all the pieces. Thank goodness they seem to have outgrown such silly ideas."

"It certainly is a lot of metal!" Ella said. "How does it feel?"

Rapunzel clanked around the stable, flexing her fingers inside the metal gauntlets. "It's heavy, but I can move a lot more easily than you'd think."

"You look just like a Charm School prince!" Rose said approvingly. "You're going to fit in perfectly."

Ella nodded in agreement.

Rapunzel grinned, but a moment later her smile

faded. "Not if I can't get over there," she said worriedly. "I still don't know how I'm going to get out of class," she reminded them. "The tournament starts on Monday and the first-years compete after lunch. Assuming I don't get knocked off my horse in the early rounds—"

"Which we're definitely assuming," Rose said.

"Then I will advance to the next day's competition with the finalists from the other years. Then on the last day the champion is decided. The tournament lasts for three days!"

Rose drummed her fingers on her waist. "Three afternoons of classes," she said thoughtfully.

"That *is* rather a lot," Ella agreed. Another yawn escaped and she covered her mouth daintily. "I'm awfully sorry," she apologized. "I'm just so sleepy."

"Me, too," Snow said from a nearby bale.

Ella turned toward Snow. She'd been so quiet that morning, Ella had nearly forgotten that Snow was in the stables, too! And she did look tired, which was a little unusual. Ella was often tired, but Snow usually had lots of pep and cheer. Now that Ella thought of it, Snow hadn't really been herself all week. *Maybe she's having trouble sleeping because she's worried for Rapunzel*, Ella thought. That would be just like Snow.

"We'll come up with something to get you out of class," Rose assured Rapunzel. "It's just a minor complication. Now, try this on so we can get the full effect."

29

She held up a helmet — the last piece of Rapunzel's armor.

Rapunzel took the helmet and set it on her head. But instead of slipping down to cover her face, it simply rested on top of her giant coils of hair.

"Let me try," Snow said. She stood on her hay bale and tried to push the helmet down from the top. It didn't budge.

"Let me help, Snow," Ella offered. But no matter how hard the two of them pushed, the helmet didn't fit.

"I think my neck is breaking," Rapunzel groaned.

"Maybe a different hairdo," Rose suggested. She and Ella restyled Rapunzel's amazingly thick, long locks into a taller, narrower coil.

"Try it now," Ella said.

Snow replaced Rapunzel's helmet, but it floated above her head like a bucket on a pole, offering no protection and no disguise.

"It's not going to work," Rapunzel said, frustrated. "It's just not big enough. And I can't use the helmet I wore at the masquerade — that was Val's."

"And it was huge," Ella reminded her. "You could barely see! You wouldn't be able to joust in that, anyway."

"It belonged to Val's great uncle Artemis," Rapunzel explained. "The man was practically a giant."

Snow started. "A giant?" she repeated, sounding a little taken aback.

"Yep," Rapunzel confirmed. "Val told me he was seven feet tall!"

Snow shivered and pulled her cape close around her shoulders. Ella peered into Snow's face. She looked . . . alarmed.

Ella leaned forward. "Snow, is everything all —"

"Ugh!" Rose groaned, still pushing on Rapunzel's head. "This helmet simply isn't going to fit."

"I'll make it fit!" Rapunzel announced. She lowered her head and prepared to ram into the stable wall to pound the thing in place.

"Not that way," Ella said gently. Together she and Rose pried the too-small headgear off of Rapunzel's head before she could give herself a concussion. "We'll just have to think of something else," Ella said. "Let's hide the rest of your gear here in the stables."

Rapunzel scowled, but after looking at her friends' faces for several moments her expression softened. Ella wasn't surprised. Rapunzel's temper often flared before her common sense had a chance to jump in. But it looked like it was finally speaking up.

"I know," Rapunzel said as Ella helped her out of her gear. "It's just another minor complication."

31

Chapter Six
Shear Misery

Rapunzel turned on her heel and walked back across her tower room. She was beginning to feel a little dizzy, but her frustration would not let her sit down. She'd been pacing for hours, pausing only to try a new hairstyle now and again in an attempt to fit the jousting helmet on her head. Each and every attempt had failed, and now her thick auburn locks dragged behind her on the floor. She had to be careful when she turned to keep from stepping on them.

Across the room, a pair of metal shears lay on the nightstand.

"No minor complication is going to keep me from proving my point to Val," she said, glaring at the scissors as though daring them to disagree. But the truth was, Rapunzel did not want to cut her hair. For though her tresses gave her fits, she secretly loved them. Her hair was thoroughly original, and often quite useful besides.

"It will grow back," she said. With a shaky hand she reached for the shears. But before she had retrieved them, a voice called her name from below.

"Rapunzel, Rapunzel, are you done with your hair?" it asked beseechingly.

Rapunzel leaned out her tower window and spotted Val below. He was standing at the edge of the forest looking up at her and holding his new lance.

"Come down," he said. "I brought my lance and I want to make sure I have mastered my balance with it before I claim my title."

Rapunzel bristled at his bravado, but felt torn. She would have loved a bit more practice with Val. Then she could be sure she could beat him at the tournament. But she couldn't reveal her moves — or the fact that she would be competing against him for real!

"How do I look?" Val asked. He knelt, holding his lance and bowing his head. It was the stance a prince would take to accept an honor — like the tournament title!

"Did I tell you my mother bought a new gown to wear to the joust?" Val went on. "I wish you could be there, too, Rapunzel." Rapunzel felt a twinge of guilt. Not only was she keeping a huge secret from Val, she also fully intended to steal his glory — and in front of his school and his family!

"Did you hear me?" Val called up. "What are you doing up there, anyway?" He rested his lance on the ground. "You're not still sore because I said you couldn't beat me, are you? You know I wish we could duel fair and square, too. I can still use your help." Then he paused, eyeing her hair. "Or are you too busy working on new hairdos for Looking Glass?"

Rapunzel scowled. "For your information I'm —" she stopped herself before uttering another word. "I just can't," she called down. "I'm busy."

Val's shoulders slumped and he thumped the end of his lance on the ground. "Oh, all right," he finally said, turning to head into the forest. Rapunzel watched him go.

"Yield at once!" he cried, aiming his lance at a large pine tree.

Rapunzel turned away from the window, more frustrated than ever. She reached for the shears for a second time. Lifting a thick lock of hair, she opened the blades and prepared to squeeze them over it. But she couldn't watch. She turned her face away. The thought of cutting off her hair was unbearable! How would her friends visit her in her tower?

Before she could force the blades together, Madame Gothel appeared in a puff of green smoke.

"Lizard's legs! What are you doing?" the witch screeched.

Rapunzel dropped the scissors and slumped down on her bed. "You startled me, Mother Gothel," she scolded. But she was actually pleased to see her foster mother. Rapunzel needed someone to talk to, and the old witch had arrived just in time.

"I need to get this helmet onto my head!" Rapunzel explained, lifting the shiny metal headpiece into the air. "There's a jousting tournament at the Charm School this week and I'm going to compete. Val said any Charm boy could beat any Princess School girl in a fair battle, and I'm going to prove him wrong!"

Madame Gothel threw her head back and cackled loudly.

Rapunzel shot her a dirty look. "Don't laugh," she said. "I'm in trouble here."

Madame Gothel gazed at her foster daughter with a gleam in her eye. "Bat's breath, dear girl," she howled. "I'm not laughing at the trouble you are *having*, I'm laughing at the trouble you'll be *causing*. I love it! You may be a princess." She shuddered. "But it appears as though I have been a perfectly wicked influence on you."

Rapunzel smirked. She couldn't deny that it was true. Madame Gothel definitely supported her feistier side. But the witch's giddiness was still not helping.

Madame Gothel gazed at Rapunzel through narrowing eyes. Her mind was hard at work. "Perhaps I can be of some help," she said. She waved her hands in the air and mumbled something about the hair of a white hare and bottomless pockets. She tapped her head with her long gnarled finger, working hard to remember something. Then she snatched the helmet, patted Rapunzel on the head, and vanished in another puff of green smoke.

Chapter Seven

Preparing for Battle

Rose watched her fairies pull away from Princess School in the family coach. Then, gathering up her skirts, she hurried down the path away from the castle school. She had to find Rapunzel as soon as possible! Last night she'd come up with the perfect solution to one of their "complications." She knew just how they could keep Rapunzel's absence a secret from the Princess School instructors.

And just in time, Rose thought as she stepped over a fallen log. The first rounds of the tournament were to begin that very day!

Rose was so busy imagining her plan in action that she didn't see Rapunzel and Val coming toward her on the path.

"Rose?" Val called out, surprised.

"Uh, hello, Val," Rose replied, giving a small curtsy. Val bowed as best he could while carrying his new lance and shield, and the threesome walked together down the path.

Rose wanted to kick herself. How could she have forgotten that Rapunzel would be walking to school with Val? She couldn't possibly tell her friend her plan in front of him. Not that Rose could have spoken if she'd wanted to. Val was so excited he was talking nonstop.

"It's finally here!" he crowed. "Only three days until I claim my title. I can't wait to don my number. Second-years get them after lunch. I hope I get a lucky one. Number, I mean. Seven, or maybe twenty. It doesn't matter, really. Today's round should be a breeze. It's the third- and fourth-years that will be tricky to beat."

Val stopped in the middle of the path and assumed a fighting pose. "I'll only be going up against class-mates today, as long as I keep winning, and four of us will get to advance. I'm sure it will be Hans, and me, and maybe Hector or Oliver, as well. Then tomorrow I can eliminate them and move on to some bigger fish!"

Like your best friend, Rose thought. Trying to keep a straight face, she turned to Rapunzel. Rose didn't have to look at the long-haired girl very carefully to know that her friend was biting her tongue — hard — to keep from speaking out.

And no wonder! thought Rose. *Val is as cocky as a rooster!* She gave Rapunzel a small smile and continued down the path ahead of the unsuited knight in shining armor and his number one foe.

"We're only to be announced by number," Val continued. "And of course everyone's faces will be hidden by the helmets. But I'm sure I'll be able to recognize each of the competitors."

Rose coughed lightly to prevent herself from laughing out loud. Rapunzel was smirking like a cat with a mouse in its mouth. She looked as though she was about to burst.

"That should be easy enough, since they will all be Charm School boys," Rapunzel said slyly.

"Indeed," Val went on. "Be they wearing helmet or not, I shall know who they are."

Rose felt her face tighten and she glanced at the giant coil of hair atop Rapunzel's head. Rapunzel had assured her that fitting her helmet over it was no longer a problem, but Rose wasn't sure how that was possible. What helmet would fit without looking ridiculous?

As the threesome turned off the forest path, the Princess School trumpets sounded.

"We'd better hurry!" Rapunzel said. "Bye, Val!" She lifted her skirts and raced off toward school.

Rose supposed Rapunzel was grateful to get away from Val. The boy was so full of himself it must have been difficult for Rapunzel not to announce her plan. Rose curtsied to the prince and hurried after Rapunzel.

"You could wish me luck," Val called after them. "Though of course I won't need it!"

"Yes, you will," Rose heard Rapunzel say under her breath.

Rose's needlepoint needle slipped through the wrong hole in her muslin. With a sigh she carefully pulled out the double stitch. All morning long she and the other Princess School students had been listening to the cheering crowd over at Charm. Though the boys and horses were hidden from view, the excitement in the air was tangible — even through the closed windows. It was terribly distracting.

"I wonder who *that* was," Ella whispered, as the clank of metal hitting metal echoed in the Stitchery chamber.

"Some poor fellow who got knocked from his horse, I'm sure!" Snow replied. Her fingers shook slightly and her own needlepoint was even messier than usual. "I hope the horse is unscathed."

Rose looked over at Rapunzel, whose muslin was completely empty. She hadn't even threaded her needle!

"Rapunzel!" Rose whispered.

Rapunzel started and looked up. Clearly she had been somewhere else in her mind. *On the back of a horse, of course*, Rose thought with a giggle.

"We're supposed to be finishing our needlepoint today, remember?" Rose said. "Maybe you should start!"

"I don't know why it's so difficult to work today." Snow sighed.

Rapunzel's gaze fell to Snow's muslin, but she didn't respond. Sometimes Snow was so oblivious!

Rose peered at Rapunzel's face. Rapunzel looked puzzled, but there was something else, a new look for the bold girl. Rapunzel looked . . . nervous.

Rose knew she would be nervous, too, if she were in Rapunzel's shoes . . . or suit of armor! Not only was she about to participate in the biggest competition of her life, she was going to do it in disguise, and skip school as well!

Out one of the tall, diamond-paned windows, Rose glimpsed the edge of a purple banner fluttering in the distance. The crowd cheered again. And then the trumpet sounded, signaling the end of Stitchery class.

Rose added two last stitches to her needlepoint, snipped the thread, and handed it to Madame Taffeta. Then she stowed her Stitchery supplies in her basket and followed her friends out of the chamber. In the corridor, princesses padded down the pink-and-white tiled floor on their way to the trunks where they kept their texts and scrolls, and to their next class.

Rose hurried to keep up with Rapunzel's purposeful stride. "Don't worry, Rapunzel," she said in a low voice. "You've been at my house every day after school and several days before sunup. You've created half a dozen new moves. *And* you're really good," she added.

"Thanks," Rapunzel said. "But I'm not worried about the competition. I'm worried about *them*." She nodded her head toward three instructors making their way down the sparkling corridor: Madame Garabaldi, Headmistress Bathilde, and Madame Lightfoot, the Self-defense teacher. Their heads were bent together in discreet but no doubt important conversation.

Rose nodded. "They do look formidable. But everything will be fine. I know my plan will work perfectly."

"Plan?" Rapunzel asked, turning to give Rose her full attention. "You have a plan?"

Rose's slender hand flew to her lips. "I forgot — I never told you!" she said. "I was going to tell you this morning — that's why I came to find you on the path. But of course Val was there. And then —"

Rapunzel tapped her foot impatiently on the floor. "Yes, yes, that's fine," she said. "Just tell me the plan!"

"The plan for what?" Snow echoed, coming up behind them.

"There's a plan?" Ella peeked over Snow's shoulder to hear.

"Shhhh!" Rapunzel said, putting a finger to her lips. Just then Hagatha and Prunilla appeared from

42

behind an ivy-carved alabaster pillar. Ella rolled her eyes. She hated running into her nasty stepsisters at school.

"Did I hear someone say 'plan'?" Hagatha sneered. "Are you planning something?"

"You forget, sister," Prunilla said to Hagatha as she eyed Ella disdainfully. "These are mere Bloomers. They couldn't think of something clever if they were captured by a giant and their lives depended on it."

"A giant?" Snow repeated, her eyes wide.

"That's right," Hagatha singsonged. "A big, hairy, princess-eating giant."

Snow gasped and put a hand to her open mouth. "There are princess-eating giants? I thought giants only enjoyed Englishmen!"

Rose glared at Ella's nasty steps. As often as she'd wished for a sister of her own, these two were reason to be gleeful about being an only child. "Come on, girls," she said flatly as she and Ella pulled Snow and Rapunzel away. "We don't want to be late for class."

"Rapunzel doesn't have to be over at Charm until the beginning of lunch," Rose whispered as they headed to Looking Glass. "We'll meet in the stables as planned and I'll tell you everything."

An hour later the girls met in their favorite lavender stall at the rear of the stables. The place was silent except for the occasional stomp of a hoof and the clank of Rapunzel's armor.

"You really look perfect," Rose said. "But what about your helmet?"

Ella looked nervous. "Yes, what about the helmet?" She wrung her hands. "And, Rapunzel, what if you get caught?"

"She won't get caught, will she, Snow?" Rose said. Rose thought they could use some of Snow's endless optimism right now. But Snow didn't respond. She was rolling a piece of hay back and forth between her pale fingers and staring into the distance. She had been that way the whole time — not even the sight of the horses seemed to pull her out of her trance.

"Are you all right, Snow?" Rose asked.

"I'm fee fi fo fum," Snow said absently. She almost sounded like she was asleep.

"What?" Ella asked.

"Snow?" Rapunzel and Rose said together.

Snow shook her head to clear it. "Oh, for goodness' sakes. What is the matter with me?" she cried. She looked around the stall at each of her friends. "How do you feel, Rapunzel?" she asked. "Are you ready for battle? Whatever will we do about the minor complications?" She stared mournfully at Rapunzel's still impossibly long locks.

"Well, I had a little help getting out of one tangle." Rapunzel pulled out her helmet with a flourish.

"Isn't that the same helmet you had last week?" Ella asked.

Rapunzel grinned. "It is the same, and yet most definitely *not* the same," she said mysteriously. "In fact it is just a tad larger. When I put it on . . ." She placed the helmet over her head and her mountain of hair magically disappeared into it, along with her face and neck. "Ta da! Having a witch for a foster mother has its perks," Rapunzel explained, her voice echoing in the helmet.

Rose couldn't see Rapunzel's mouth, but could tell by her voice that she was grinning. She felt a tingle of excitement. Rapunzel was completely and appropriately suited, and it was time to go!

"Oh, Rapunzel!" Snow said, clapping her hands together in delight.

"Okay, so we're almost ready," Rose said, getting back to business.

"But what about the other minor complication? Isn't Madame Lightfoot going to know something is amiss when Rapunzel doesn't show up for class?" Ella asked. She was wringing her hands again.

"Don't worry," Rose said confidently. She held up a handful of hay and the dress Rapunzel had taken off to don the Charm School uniform. "If all goes well, nobody will even know Rapunzel is gone!"

Chapter Eight

Facing Off

With a loud clank, Rapunzel ducked around the last rose hedge separating Princess School from The Charm School for Boys. Then, poking her helmeted head over the top, she snuck one last peek at Princess School. Framed in one of the diamond-paned windows on the second floor she saw three dainty hands waving to her from the lunch chamber. Rapunzel waved her own metal-sheathed hand back, cringing at the sound. Armor might be good for jousting but it certainly was not good for sneaking.

Luckily the sneaking part of her adventure was over for now. Moving away from the hedge, Rapunzel clanked the last few steps onto Charm territory. She felt her heart hammer in her chest as she surveyed the surroundings.

The Charm School grounds had been transformed into an enormous jousting arena. Two sets of bleachers lined a long jousting run. It looked like a long grassy lane with gates on the edges to keep competitors from veering. Stables were positioned at either end of the run, and nearby were large corrals where squires were holding horses. Scribes on ladders hurriedly penned the standings onto giant scrolls. The entire place was crawling with Charm boys in full armor. The field and stands were filled with the glimmer of metal.

Wasting no time, Rapunzel quickly lost herself in the crowd beside a nearby squire's table. The boy behind it was wearing a floppy green and purple beret that kept drooping into his eyes as he handed numbers to first-year princes in full armor.

Perfect, she thought. *He won't look twice at me.*

With a start, Rapunzel noticed that the timid squire had only a few numbers left. She stepped boldly in front of a rather tall first-year boy and snatched the number 17 from the squire's hand.

"Pardon me," Rapunzel excused herself, speaking as low as she could. "I have been waiting forever," she said to the prince she pushed past.

Though he said nothing, Rapunzel could tell by his stance that the prince was annoyed by her brash behavior. He leaned over, trying to get a look at her number.

Probably taking stock so he can knock me out of my seat later, she thought. *Well, he can try!*

Before the squire or the prince could say anything, Rapunzel clanged back out of the line. It would not be good to call more attention to herself than was necessary.

As she made her way toward the stables to find her mount and her gear, Rapunzel felt a tiny twinge of guilt. Abrupt or pushy behavior wasn't acceptable for any prince — or princess. Plus, there was a chance that her competing would prevent a Charm School prince from doing the same, which didn't seem fair.

Maybe they have extra numbers, she thought. *And anyway, I had to get one somehow. I've come too far to turn back.*

With her head down and the number clutched in her fist, Rapunzel finally spotted her stall. It was plain on the outside, but inside it held a lance and shield, and most important, a horse. The chestnut Morgan mare nickered as Rapunzel clanked inside. A golden plate with the horse's name carved into it hung over her feedbag: RIGHTEOUS.

Rapunzel leaned in close to the mare's ear. She felt a little bit like Snow as she whispered into the beast's soft fur. "I'm Rapunzel," she said. "And I'm glad you're a girl, too." She didn't think it would do any good to keep her secret from her partner on the field. "We are going to be a great team."

Quickly Rapunzel collected her shield and banged her way toward the enormous hanging scrolls. She needed to see whom she was up against, and when.

Looking through her visor she ran her eyes down the columns of numbers. She found hers, 17, and beside it a 4. The winner of her first duel would then face off with number 8.

First 4 then 8. They sound easy enough to defeat, she thought. Then she smiled to herself; 4 and 8 could be anyone! Well, any of the first-year competitors. For the first two rounds of the tournament, all of the jousters only faced opponents in the same age bracket. Rapunzel was pleased she would get to warm up with the youngest boys.

With a fanfare of trumpets, the first pair of princes was led to the field by purple- and green-clad squires. At the same time, the next several pairs were announced so that they would have time to mount up. Numbers 4 and 17 would be on deck soon! Her heart racing, Rapunzel led Righteous to the holding corral and scanned the other jousters swarming out of the stable area. She wanted to sneak a look at 4 before she was galloping toward him. But the field was so crowded it was like looking for a needle in a haystack.

"I need a better vantage point," Rapunzel said to Righteous. She stepped into the stirrup and swung her other leg easily over the mare's back. All her practice had paid off. Even in the heavy armor she was a graceful rider.

Seated on the back of her horse, Rapunzel peered

toward the far side of the jousting field. She hardly paid attention to the princes who were clashing and clattering to the ground. At last she saw a red 4 on a suit of bronze armor. It was hard to tell but 4 seemed to be sizing her up, too. His head swung back. Was he laughing? Rapunzel looked at the red 17 on her breast plate. She did make a rather small boy.

Then before she knew it, a squire had taken Righteous' reigns and was leading her to the jousting field. She was up!

"Let's show these boys how it's done," Rapunzel whispered in her horse's ear. The squire handed up her lance and shield. Then the flag in the center of the field dropped. Without even thinking, Rapunzel nudged Righteous' flanks and the two went flying toward the bronze knight with lance raised. Rapunzel was barely aware of the wind rushing against her helmet. She stared straight ahead, her eyes locked on her opponent. When they met, Rapunzel was aware of a firm *thump*, but barely stirred in her seat. She turned to see Number 4 lying flat on his back on the field. She had dismounted the prince while hardly trying! He lifted his visor and looked grudgingly up at her from the muddy grass. His face was unfamiliar, but clearly he wasn't laughing now.

After they nodded to each other to acknowledge the end of the duel, Rapunzel could not help herself. She giggled as she watched Number 4 scramble to his feet and lead his horse off the field. His bottom was covered in mud and bits of grass. This was easier than she'd imagined.

To the delight of the cheering crowd watching from the stands, Rapunzel unseated Number 8 almost as quickly. She was ready with one of her new moves, but could tell on her approach that 8 would not require it. He was having difficulty staying on his horse even during his approach! She banked the move for later and toppled him with a simple blow.

These princes may be charming, but they aren't very skilled, Rapunzel thought. As she watched the next few pairs spar she actually found herself wishing her potential opponents posed more of a challenge. If it weren't for the thrill of her illegal entry, she might have found the first day of competiton a little . . . boring! At least now, after winning her first two rounds, she would start to face off against some older boys. Of course, any older boys she faced would be working their way down, not up. Every prince got two chances on the first day of battle. But once a competitor lost two jousts he was out and had to sit in the stands with the parents and instructors.

Rapunzel scanned the seated crowd. The stands were fuller than they had been, but of course Val was not there.

Rapunzel drummed her metal-clad fingers on her

shield. She was ready to win her final battle and get back to class! All she needed to do was win one more in order to come back and compete tomorrow.

Finally, 17 was again called to the field. Rapunzel gave Righteous a pat and shouldered her lance. She barely bothered to look at the boy she was about to face, Number 12.

"Do hurry," she mumbled as her opponent struggled with his shield and lance. He was taking forever to mount. "I could blow him over from here," she told Righteous. "He's no more a challenge than the scarecrow — and almost as skinny." Rapunzel laughed quietly. Suddenly the laugh stuck in her throat. The boy really was as skinny and tall as the scarecrow — and there was only one prince she knew who fit that description. It had to be Dap! For a moment Rapunzel felt proud. Dap hadn't been eliminated yet! Then she felt bad. He was on his way out, competing with first-years. It had to be his last run, and she was going to be the one to force him out.

The flag dropped.

"Easy," Rapunzel said as she spurred Righteous on. She aimed for a spot in the center of Dap's shield — a spot that she knew wouldn't hurt him too much. She connected with a bang and winced as she heard Dap connect next with the muddy field behind her.

Turning Righteous, Rapunzel stole a glance back.

Another prince, Number 5, had come out onto the field to offer Dap a hand. To Rapunzel's relief, Dap got to his feet easily. He was completely fine, just muddy. She almost laughed — and the knight beside Dap did. It was a laugh Rapunzel knew well. She had spotted Val at last. He was Number 5.

Though a minute earlier Rapunzel had been ready to get back to Princess School, now that the time had come, she wanted to stall. Rapunzel led Righteous back to her stall slowly so she could watch the final joust of the day. It was Number 13 versus Number 5 — Val. Both princes looked secure in their saddles. They both had excellent form. Their lances were steady as their horses picked up speed.

"Perfect!" Rapunzel said out loud as Val shifted his weight and caught 13 off guard in the upper right corner of his shield. It was a maneuver Rapunzel knew well — she had taught Val how to do it. Number 13 wavered, then slipped to the side. He could not recover his balance and leaped off his horse to save himself the embarrassment of landing on his rump.

I'll bet that's Allister Arlington, Rapunzel thought as she led Righteous to her stall. Allister had been Ella's penprince in Cordial Correspondence class — and he was supposed to be one of the more talented jousters at Charm. Rapunzel couldn't help feeling proud of Val's victory.

Inside the stall, Rapunzel patted Righteous. "Thank you," she whispered. "See you tomorrow."

She slipped as quietly as she could toward the arena exit. She didn't want to get noticed now, and was also trying to hear the standings announced over the sound of her own clattering armor.

"First- and second-year princes advancing to tomorrow's heats will be Numbers 26, 32, 3, 11, 9, 17, 5, and 14," a scribe shouted. The crowd cheered and Rapunzel smiled. *Number 14 must be Hans Charming,* she thought. She had no idea who the other advancing first-years were but felt certain she could unseat any of them fairly easily.

Taking a quick look behind her, Rapunzel prepared to hop the rosebush. She checked her step in midair and fell clumsily to the other side. Val and Dap were walking right behind her!

"I knew you'd advance," Dap said, clanging Val on the back.

Val nodded. "And I knew you wouldn't." He laughed. Dap laughed with him. "I just wish Rapunzel were here to see this," Val said. "Her moves are perfect! Did you see me take down Allister? I can't wait to tell her."

Beneath her helmet, Rapunzel felt her face go hot.

Chapter Nine

No Dummy

Snow adjusted her arm around "Rapunzel" and walked down the hall as naturally as she could. "I hope Madame Garabaldi is on the other side of the castle," she whispered over "Rapunzel's" head to Rose.

"Me, too," Rose whispered back. She was holding up the other side of the dummy they had made using Rapunzel's dress and a whole lot of straw. Ella walked behind them, making sure nothing came loose.

Snow had to admit that "Rapunzel" looked pretty good. She was the right size, was wearing the right clothes, and thanks to her long skirts, nobody could tell the stuffed bloomer legs under her dress were not walking on their own. They should be able to convince everyone that Rapunzel was still with them — as long as nobody asked why Rapunzel was wearing a veil over her head. Or expected her to speak. Or move on her own. Or . . .

Snow shook her head. She couldn't think about their ruse anymore. It was too alarming.

A giant yawn escaped Snow's lips as she tried to keep pace with Rose's quick steps. She had been so sleepy lately. She could barely keep up with her course work . . . or even her friends' conversations. She blinked rapidly as she listened to the chatter of other princesses in the hallway, and suddenly the strange refrain that had been haunting her lately echoed in her head once more — "fee fi fo fum."

Snow's sleepy eyes grew wide again and she looked around. "Where is that coming from?" she mumbled.

Rose and Ella looked blankly back at Snow. They obviously hadn't said — or heard — anything. Why was it stuck in her head? Was it one of Gruff's rumbling tunes? Snow felt a chill snaking its way up her neck. Maybe it was another piece of the strange dreams she'd been having lately!

With her free hand, Snow rubbed her eyes. Every night for a week she had been going to bed early, exhausted, letting the dwarves finish the dishes alone. And though she always went right to sleep, her dreams had been so vivid and odd that when she woke up she felt as if she hadn't slept at all.

Even more confusing was that Snow was convinced the strange dreams were coming true! First she dreamed of oatmeal. And then, the next morning at breakfast, there was oatmeal on the table! Instead of eating, Snow had hurried out to the henhouse to start her morning chores. Dreams that came true were supposed to be good things, but Snow would rather her dreams remain just that: dreams. At least the ones she'd been having lately.

In the henhouse things were even stranger. She was collecting the eggs like she usually did when she noticed something amiss.

A lovely tan hen with dark speckles on its shoulders and feet was nesting alongside the others. Snow was absolutely certain that she had never seen this bird in the coop before. She named each of the new chicks shortly after they hatched, and never forgot a beak.

"Well, hello!" Snow greeted, trying to sound cheerful in spite of the uneasy feeling she was having. She wouldn't want the poor hen to feel unwelcome. "Where did you come from?"

As soon as the words were out of her mouth, Snow's pale hand flew to her lips. She suddenly remembered — she had dreamed about the hen the night before! And now, here it was — a brand-new bantam sitting in one of the nests.

"Did I bring you here by dreaming of you?" she whispered. "I couldn't have. All I did was lie down in my bed and close my eyes!"

The hen's beady yellow eyes were unblinking as it

wiggled in its nest. Snow reached beneath the hen and pulled out . . . a golden egg!

The poor girl had nearly swooned as she'd placed the egg in her basket. Then, so she wouldn't worry the dwarves, she'd slipped the egg into her pocket. The new hen had to be ill to lay such an egg. Snow had told herself she would check up on the bird after school, and hurried back inside.

Just remembering the golden egg made Snow feel woozy again. She stumbled and Ella caught her arm. "Are you okay?" Ella asked kindly.

Snow hadn't wanted to breathe a word to the dwarves about her strange nights and her powerful dreams, but she thought maybe she should tell her friends.

"I feel like I haven't slept in days," she began.

Ella nodded sympathetically. Snow was about to go on when she was interrupted by a voice behind them.

"Ella, Snow, Rapunzel, and Rose," Arinda, the miller's daughter, exclaimed. "I always see you four together. Why, you're practically joined at the hip!" She laughed.

Snow laughed with her, her arm tightening around the fake Rapunzel's waist. "Practically!" she answered. If only the girl knew!

"Rapunzel, is that a new hairdo you're hiding?" Arinda asked. She bent down to look under Rapunzel's veil. Snow had to move quickly to keep her from seeing the ball of straw underneath.

"Bad hair day," Rose whispered, putting her finger to her lips.

The miller's daughter nodded knowingly. "Good thing she has a loyal friend like you, Beauty," Arinda whispered and backed off.

Gently, Ella nudged Snow down the corridor to the left. "That was close," she murmured.

Snow nodded. She had to keep her mind on the dummy if they were going to keep their friend out of trouble. She adjusted her arm around the fake Rapunzel and made a secret wish that the real Rapunzel would be back soon. And unharmed!

The three girls and their makeshift friend crowded through the wide door and into the Self-defense classroom. The chamber was already set up with large props depicting a forest. "Let's sit behind that prop," Rose suggested. She pointed the way toward a large tree on the side of the room.

"Good idea." Ella nodded and the girls steered "Rapunzel" to the far side of the chamber and sat down at the base of the tree, tucking her in behind a clump of bushes.

"Whew!" Rose said, dabbing her face with a lace handkerchief. "This is tricky."

Ella looked around at the other Bloomers getting ready for class. No one seemed to be looking at them. "So far, so good," she said softly. "Let's hope it's going as well at Charm."

Snow took a breath. While "Rapunzel" was resting safely, she wanted to try again to tell Ella and Rose how strange she was feeling.

"There's something going on," she began.

"I'll say," Rose agreed. "Right this very minute Rapunzel is masquerading as a Charm School boy!" She and Ella laughed.

"No, I mean in my dreams —" Snow tried again, but as soon as the words were out of her mouth, Madame Lightfoot strode into the classroom. The tall teacher swung her long silver braid over her shoulder and clapped her hands together to get the girls' attention.

"Today we will work on darting and dodging," Madame Lightfoot said. "These moves may seem simple, but perfecting them can be quite difficult. Yet we must aspire to do so, for they are particularly useful when one is being pursued by a large creature such as an ogre or a giant."

Snow went cold. What was it about giants? The very word had been giving her the cold shivers lately. Hearing it again now, she realized she had been dreaming of more than oatmeal and chickens. There had been a giant in her dreams, too. A scary one! And if her dreams were starting to come true . . .

Snow's hand flew to her mouth to stifle a gasp. She masked the noise, but lost her grip on "Rapunzel." With another sharp intake of breath she grabbed for the dummy's arm. All she got was a fistful of hay!

Luckily Ella was still beside her. Pushing Snow aside, Ella threw the doll to the floor and dropped to her knees next to it. Then with a quick tug she pulled Snow's skirt until she was kneeling down beside her.

"Are you hurt, Rapunzel?" Ella asked loudly, jabbing the dummy in the ribs. Snow could not speak. She simply stared wide-eyed at Ella. "Just play along," Ella whispered to Snow. "Of course we can take you to the nurse, right, Madame Lightfoot?" Without waiting for an answer, Ella pulled "Rapunzel" to her feet. Rose grabbed the other side and together she and Ella shouldered their friend out of the room.

Snow followed two steps behind, still holding a fistful of straw.

Chapter Ten
Princess in the Straw

Without her armor, Rapunzel felt light as a feather. But back inside Princess School and still dressed in her Charm School uniform, she knew she was as conspicuous as a peacock!

Rapunzel charged down the corridor as quickly as she could. She was not sure how she was going to alert her friends that she was back — and needed her dress! She just knew she had to do it fast.

Rounding the corner, she skidded to a halt. The door to Self-defense was opening. Rapunzel turned to start running the other way, but was quickly overtaken by Snow, Ella, Rose, and her other self.

"Little Princesses' room. Fast!" Ella hissed.

"Are we ever glad to see you!" Rose whispered as they tumbled inside the elegant bathroom. "How'd you do?"

"It was a piece of tart!" Rapunzel started to brag.

"Those boys went down easier than chocolate pudding." She assumed a jousting pose to demonstrate. "You should have seen —"

"We don't have time for details," Ella interrupted, pulling Rapunzel's tunic over her head. Rose and Snow were already unstuffing Rapunzel's dress. Straw flew everywhere. It stuck in the girls' hair and scratched Rapunzel's neck as she pulled her dress over her head.

Rose had just finished buttoning the back of the gown when the girls heard footsteps in the corridor. A moment later the door opened and Madame Lightfoot stepped inside.

"I looked for you in the nurse's chamber but she said you hadn't been there." Madame Lightfoot looked concerned and confused as she surveyed the straw-strewn room. "Are you all right?" she asked.

Rapunzel looked at Ella and saw her swallow hard. She wished she'd thought to ask why they were in such a hurry to get out of Self-defense!

"Just fine," Rapunzel beamed. Out of the corner of her eye she spotted her Charm uniform crumpled on the floor. Discreetly she slid her foot out and pulled the garments under her skirt, but not before Madame Lightfoot looked down.

Without even glancing at the mirror Rapunzel could tell her face was flushed. She stepped forward.

The jousting had gone well, but she knew it would take a miracle to be able to leave Princess School to compete tomorrow and the next day. The game was up.

Rapunzel had barely opened her mouth to repair what damage she could when Madame Lightfoot smiled. "I am glad to see you're all right, my dear," the instructor said. "Though I'm not quite sure what transpired." She raised an eyebrow.

Rapunzel's friends all spoke at once. "A splinter," said Rose.

"She fainted," Snow piped in.

"She tripped," Ella offered.

"I, uh, tripped, got a splinter, and fainted," Rapunzel explained, feeling a glimmer of hope grow within her. If she weren't so nervous she would have laughed out loud. All of this fuss over a supposed splinter, and she had just faced and defeated three armed knights!

Madame Lightfoot looked each of the girls in the eye in turn. Rapunzel noticed Snow fidgeting uncomfortably and felt a flash of guilt for having gotten them all in trouble.

"I suppose the important thing is that you're unharmed," the teacher said. "I have been meaning to speak to you privately, Rapunzel. However, since this will pertain to all of you I will speak of the matter now." Looking even taller than usual, she folded her arms across her chest. "I believe the four of you are well aware that the grand jousting tournament is being conducted at the Charm School at this very moment," she said slowly.

Rapunzel tried not to wince. She could tell Madame Lightfoot was looking at her for a reaction. She opened her eyes a bit wider and nodded slightly, hoping it was the right thing to do.

The teacher continued. "I happened to see an impassioned plea on Lady Bathilde's desk asking that the girls at Princess School be allowed to observe the tournament. But I had no idea —"

Rapunzel released her held breath in a whoosh. That was what this was about! "It was bold, I know," Rapunzel interrupted to apologize. She had hastily penned the request ages ago when all she had wanted was to watch Val compete in the tournament. Of course she'd assumed her request would be fruitless but she'd had to try. And she certainly never expected it to draw attention to the fact that she was competing herself! "I should not have wasted the Headmistress' time." Rapunzel hung her head and buried her calloused palms in her skirts.

"It was bold, indeed," Madame Lightfoot said. She did not sound mad. In fact, she sounded delighted. "That is why I wanted you to be the first to know that Lady Bathilde has granted your request! The entire school will watch the remainder of the competition from the Charm School bleachers!"

Rapunzel looked at her friends. This was better news than they could have imagined! It would be much easier to sneak out of the bleachers than it was to sneak out of class. As long as her armor concealed her identity, the competition could continue — with her in it!

Rose, Ella, and Snow sandwiched Rapunzel in a hug. "That's wonderful!" Rose said. She was practically jumping up and down.

Madame Lightfoot smiled, and her green eyes twinkled. "Now, back to class."

Ella held the door open to make sure Madame Lightfoot left first. The instructor glanced back once as she led the girls into the hall. Rapunzel paused to scratch her ankle and scoop her uniform up under her arm. On her way out the door she heard Madame Lightfoot mumble something about the cleaning staff. "They really ought to do a better job," she said. "It looks like a stable in there."

Chapter Eleven

Fears and Fanfare

"I can't believe we're actually here!" Ella swept her skirts under her before daintily taking a seat on the bleachers beside Snow and Rose. She looked out across the jousting field. "Isn't it exciting?"

"I wish I was Rapunzel's squire. I can barely sit still," Rose said.

"How are *you* doing?" Ella whispered toward her feet. From beneath the bleachers, Rapunzel's muffled voice answered back.

"I'm just fine," she grunted. "Except for all of these blasted buckles! I wish Rose was my squire, too!"

Ella and Rose giggled at their struggling friend. Then Ella's expression grew serious.

"Shhhh," she whispered. "We don't want the teachers to notice you've disappeared!"

"Hold on, Rapunzel," Rose said. "I'll be right down." After making sure none of the Princess School teachers was looking, Rose slipped between the bleacher boards to the dark spot where Rapunzel was attempting to don her armor.

"Ella, keep your eyes peeled," Rose instructed.

Ella nodded. This kind of sneaking around was much more fun than sneaking around her stepmother! Still, she was full of nervous excitement.

Ella nudged Snow, who was sitting silently beside her. "You haven't said a word, Snow. Aren't you pleased to be out of class? You must think the horses are beautiful, at least."

Snow blinked like she was just waking up. "Hmmm? Oh. Sorry. I'm just sleepy, I guess."

"Sleepy" didn't exactly describe just how disoriented Snow had seemed lately. But Ella didn't have time to press. On the field the mock battles were ending and the squires were calling out the numbers of the competitors for the first heat.

"Hurry up, Rapunzel," Ella whispered. "You're up next!"

"The pins and buckles on this armor are impossible!" Rapunzel said, loudly this time.

Rose hushed her, but not quickly enough. Several princesses sitting nearby began to peer through the cracks between the boards beneath their slippers. And Ella saw them leaning close to one another and whispering.

For a moment Ella felt panicked. If anyone told Lady Bathilde or Madame Garabaldi what Rapunzel was up to, today's competition would be over before it began! But the only girls who had seen were Bloomers — and they wouldn't rat on Rapunzel. Or at least Ella hoped not.

Ella put her finger to her lips to show the girls sitting next to them that she was about to tell them a secret. "Rapunzel is our undercover champion," she whispered. "If she wins, all of the Bloomers will share the grand reward."

A ripple of excitement passed through the crowd of Bloomers. Ella hoped the secret would stay in their class. If Hagatha and Prunilla discovered what they were up to, the result could be horrible.

Beside her, Rose reemerged and took her seat as if she'd only just stood to wave at a friend across the field. She caught the worried look on Ella's face and whispered to the Bloomers on the other side. "Keep it amongst the Bloomers," she hissed. "It's our first-year secret."

Some of them smiled and clapped their hands together excitedly. Others stared, wide-eyed, as if just the thought of such a thing was impossible. Ella didn't particularly care what they thought. She only hoped they could all keep it under wraps.

"I do have a nice riding cape," she heard Scarlet

Hood muse nearby. "And I never get to wear it. Farthingdale would be just the place! Do you really think we'll get access?"

"As long as we don't betray her cover, it's almost a certainty!" Ella assured her calmly. But inside she was not so convinced.

Just then, she spotted a figure striding across the field toward a stall with a fine-looking mare. Number 17 looked like a knight. She could fight like one, Ella knew, but Ella had no idea if they would actually allow a bunch of princesses into Farthingdale if she won.

"Look there." Rose pointed. Across from them in the Charm stands, Dap waved wildly. "I guess he's not competing anymore."

He certainly didn't look disappointed about it. He was waving like a madman. Demurely, Ella flicked her handkerchief in his direction. He didn't seem to notice.

"Better say hello before he injures himself!" Ella said, giving him a proper wave.

Rose waved her own lace hanky, but in spite of the excitement Snow had fallen asleep on Rose's shoulder.

"Look, Snow, there's Val. Didn't Rapunzel say he was Number 5?"

Prince Valerian cantered up and down on the other side of the course, taking practice runs on his horse and perfecting his humble victory wave.

"He certainly looks confident." Rose giggled.

The whisperings in the Bloomer section subsided when Number 17 rode out of the stables.

"She looks perfect — just like a champion!" Ella said quietly.

"She *is* a champion," Rose replied. "And she's going to win, I'm certain of it."

Ella wished she felt as certain. She believed in her friend, of course. But many of the Charm School boys had been riding horses and wielding lances since they were tykes. And all of this deception made her feel nervous.

The Bloomers applauded a little more loudly as 17 galloped past the stands to take her place.

A squire led Rapunzel's horse to the starting line. Then, without ado, Rapunzel was galloping toward her opponent, Number 14, with her lance held firmly in front of her. Ella wanted to close her eyes as the riders met. With a clash of metal, Rapunzel's lance collided with the other knight's shield and he dropped to the ground like an overripe pear.

Ella released the breath she did not know she had been holding. "They go down easier than chocolate pudding," she murmured, repeating Rapunzel's words from the day before.

Snow was still snoozing on Rose, but the rest of the Bloomers were applauding more loudly than ever. Ella hoped the instructors who sat in the booths at the front of the stands would not question their extra enthusiasm. She could hardly blame them for it.

"I knew she was good, but I didn't know she was *this* good!" Ella gently shook Snow awake. She may have been tired but she couldn't miss this. "You may be able to meet the horses from Farthingdale Stables after all, Snow!" She tried to sound extra sure of herself in spite of her doubts. She simply had to say something to cheer up her poor pale friend. Ella raised her eyebrows and looked into Snow's sleepy face. She waited for the smile to appear on Snow's ruby red lips. What happened instead was more shocking than Rapunzel's easy victory.

Snow White burst into tears.

Chapter Twelve
Clashing Thoughts

Lowering her lance, Rapunzel let Righteous slow to a trot as she approached the end of the field. If Number 14 was Hans Charming, he needed to get a few more tips from that uncle of his. He teetered on his mount like a top!

It felt good to be on Righteous' back again — natural, even in heavy armor. With her friends watching and cheering her on, not even the thought of facing the older princes could make her tense. Rapunzel looked quickly at the bleachers and saw Ella and Rose huddled around Snow. They had been watching, hadn't they?

She resisted the urge to wave and instead turned her mind back to the joust. It was so exhilarating!

"I think this is the most fun I have had in my life," Rapunzel whispered to Righteous. It was true, but she wasn't exactly sure why. Was it the speed? The danger? The feeling of victory? Whatever it was, it all added up to a strong sense of freedom. Rapunzel grinned beneath her helmet. "It's just like me to feel free locked in a metal cage of armor." She patted her horse and swung her around to watch the next heat.

Numbers 20 and 23 came together fast in a clash of lances and armor. Even Rapunzel had to cringe. The sound was horrendous and both jousters landed on the muddy field with a squelching *thunk*.

"I'm sure glad I stay on," Rapunzel murmured. Watching this closely she could barely believe she was doing the same thing these clashing knights were. "They don't have much style, do they?" she asked Righteous as the next pair ran headlong into each other. "They make it look so painful!"

In spite of the awkwardness of the Charm boys, Rapunzel was riveted. She simply loved everything about jousting . . . even the ridiculous armor that sat heavy and hot on her shoulders!

Rapunzel was starting to feel a little dazed when the next heat was announced. It was one of Val's!

Val's armor gleamed silver. His horse was pure white, and Rapunzel grudgingly nodded her approval. He sat well in his saddle, and he had reason to feel secure. He was indeed one of the finest jousters at the competition.

At the other end of the field Rapunzel spotted Hans Charming whispering to Val's opponent, a much larger knight dressed in black armor, like his own. "That must be his brother, Lars!" Rapunzel told Righteous. "He's the favored champion."

Rapunzel felt torn. She wanted Val to win, but was it just so she could beat him later?

Righteous nickered and tossed her head as Val spurred his mount. She seemed as excited about the match as Rapunzel.

The larger knight advanced, holding his lance steady and barely moving in his saddle. He picked up speed. Instead of looking larger as he approached, Val started to look smaller by comparison.

The clash was tremendous. Both knights took a hit and it looked like they would both stay on to charge each other again. Then, at the last possible moment, Val leaned in behind his shield and managed to strike a second blow with the corner of the plate metal — a little desperation tactic Rapunzel had taught him.

When the black knight took a dive into the mud, Rapunzel nearly cheered. She was so proud. Val had knocked out the defending champion! As Val did a victory lap, waving at all of the princesses in the stands, she spotted his parents. Queen Valerian looked impeccable in her new gown. And the king could not have puffed his chest out another inch. They were even prouder!

Inside, Rapunzel felt her emotions colliding with

jousting-level impact. She tore her eyes from Val, slid off of Righteous, and walked to the scrolls to check the standings. Val was her friend, but he was also her competition. Perhaps her fiercest. She couldn't cheer him on if she wanted to beat him, could she?

Rapunzel slid a gauntleted finger down the list of competitors. Her heart hammered. Then it skipped a beat altogether.

Before her lay the possibility of her greatest hope and her worst fear. If Val won once more today — and she won just twice — they might face each other in the final tomorrow.

It's what you've been waiting for, isn't it? she told herself as she walked back to her horse. *A fair competition?*

"Of course it is," Rapunzel whispered to Righteous. She imagined the look on Val's face when she pulled off her helmet and he realized she had been competing against him and all the Charm princes. The old Val would laugh and clap her soundly on the back. But what about the new, proud Val? What would he think?

He's still Val, and Val can take a joke, Rapunzel assured herself. *Besides, he has to learn that a princess is nothing to sneeze at.*

Rapunzel's number was called, pulling her out of her thoughts and back to the field.

"There's no use sitting around pondering possibilities, Righteous. We have a joust to win!" But even as she defeated yet another prince, she could not unseat the biggest fear in her head. Would Val forgive her for stealing such a public and anticipated honor? Might she be sending their friendship crashing into the mud right along with her friend?

Rapunzel wished she could shake her own mane the way Righteous did. Maybe it would clear her head of all her unwanted thoughts. She needed to remember what got her into this armor in the first place.

"He refused to face me in a fair fight," she whispered as much to herself as to her horse. "He said no prince would ever take on a princess, much less lose to her." Rapunzel nodded her heavy helmeted head and felt her resolve return. "The valiant Prince Val has more to learn than a few jousting moves. And I am just the princess for the job."

Chapter Thirteen
Spilling the Beans

"What's wrong, Snow?" Ella asked, gently wiping a tear from her friend's face.

Rose turned her attention away from the field. "You've got to tell us what's going on," she encouraged.

Snow felt her bottom lip begin to quiver and bit it to hold it still. "I'm not sure," she said. "That's just the trouble!"

"Start at the beginning," Ella coached.

Snow took a deep breath and sat up a little straighter. "I just feel so . . . so . . . out of sorts," she said. "No matter how much sleep I get at night, I wake up tired and sore. My legs ache and my arms feel like I've been hauling firewood for the cook stove all night." Snow felt her eyes welling with a fresh batch of tears. "And then there are my dreams," she cried. "I think they're coming true!"

Ella massaged Snow's arm gently. "Tell us about the dreams," she said softly.

"First I dreamed about a chicken, and the next morning when I went to gather eggs, there was a new hen in the henhouse! And the day after that I was in the garden picking flowers and singing a song I'd heard somewhere, when a harp in the garden shed started singing along!"

"A harp?" Rose repeated, obviously confused.

"Was singing along?" Ella finished.

"It sounds like a strange sort of magic," Rose said thoughtfully.

Ella's eyebrows knit together. "You don't think it has something to do with Malodora, do you?" she whispered with a shudder.

Snow gasped at the mention of her horrible stepmother's name and her eyes brimmed with tears yet again. Malodora was headmistress at the nearby Grimm School for witches. She had used her magic against Snow many times before. "I hadn't thought of that!" Snow wailed.

Just then the crowd cheered as a competitor clad in polished armor took the field.

"It's Val again!" Ella cried.

Snow sat up straighter to get a better view of the field. Still, she couldn't see clearly — her vision was blurred by her damp eyes.

The flag dropped and Val raced down the field on his regal-looking mount. His lance was steady as the horse galloped at full speed toward his opponent, a wiry-looking prince in dented armor. Then, moments before he was to clash with the other boy, Val moved the lance to his opposite hand. His opponent was left with no time to compensate. Val's lance struck him squarely on the left side of his shield, sending the boy tumbling to the ground.

The crowd cheered wildly. "Go, Val!" Rose shouted, leaping to her feet with abandon.

"How unprincesslike of you, Rose," Ella scolded with a smile. "Besides, we're supposed to be cheering for Rapunzel."

"We are," Rose replied with a grin. "She was Val's coach!"

Snow smiled weakly at her friends' banter. She knew she should be thrilled to be at the tournament, to be watching all these beautiful horses and their riders compete — and to be out of school! But things felt so topsy-turvy that she was numb. And she was so, so tired. She just didn't have the energy to root for anyone — not even one of her best friends.

With a huge sigh Snow gazed at the muddy field. Rapunzel was preparing to ride again — this time against a tall boy in a silvery-blue armor.

"This one looks formidable," Ella whispered.

Rose nodded. "If Rapunzel wins this time, it means

she rides in the championship rounds tomorrow!" she said as the flag dropped. "Just like Val!"

Snow felt a lump rise in her throat. She gripped Ella's and Rose's hands.

A hush fell over the crowd as the two knights thundered toward each other.

The sound of the horses' pounding hooves echoed in Snow's head, and she was suddenly reminded of other pounding footsteps from her dream — those of a giant!

What if I conjure up a giant? she thought. *The whole kingdom would be in danger . . . and it would be all my fault!* Her whole body quivered at the thought. She had been dreaming about one, she was sure of it. Just like the oatmeal and the harp and the hen!

On the field, Rapunzel and her opponent came together in a clash and crash of metal, with both striking each other in the center of their shields. Snow gasped as Rapunzel lost her balance for a moment but clung to the saddle with her legs. The silver-blue knight did the same. Neither fell. They would have to face off again.

Snow nearly covered her eyes as Rapunzel and her opponent prepared to thunder toward each other for a second time. It looked so painful! What if the horses got hurt? Worse, what if Rapunzel got hurt?

Beside her, Ella and Rose were leaning forward eagerly.

The flag dropped, and the horses heaved themselves across the field again. Both riders held their lances steady and level. They were nearly upon each other when Raunzel crouched down in her saddle and lowered her lance, striking near the waist. The older boy was so startled he nearly dropped his shield. Rapunzel turned and struck him again on the shoulder, more lightly this time, and the Charm boy fell to the muddy field.

The spectators went wild. Bloomers leaped to their feet, nearly colliding with one another. On the other side of the field, the boys in the Charm School bleachers jumped up, whooping loudly. This was an upset! The armored prince on the ground was none other than the much touted fourth year, Emmett Pantaloon!

"She did it!" Ella cried, nearly stepping on Rose's foot.

"Of course she did," Rose said, her voice full of pride.

"Of course," Ella agreed as she sat down again next to Snow. She peered at Snow's pale, blotchy face. "Now tell us more about this strange magic," she coaxed.

Snow shook her head. "I don't know what to tell you," she admitted. She felt utterly overwhelmed. "When I go to sleep I start to dream, first of large green leaves, and climbing — always climbing. Then things get stranger.

And when I wake up some of the things from my dreams have come true." Snow sobbed. "But I never thought a dream come true would be like this. I haven't told the dwarves because I don't want them to worry. But on top of it all I'm afraid the new hen isn't well. Just look at this!"

Snow pulled the golden egg out of her pocket.

Rose and Ella stared at the egg in Snow's hand. It shimmered softly in the afternoon sunlight.

Snow sniffled and dabbed at her eyes. "I thought I dreamed it, but then I found it right in her nest. My dreams are all coming true. And some of them are nightmares!"

Chapter Fourteen
Mystery Solved

Rapunzel led Righteous into her stall and gave her a carrot she'd pulled from Madame Gothel's garden and stashed in her armor. "Thanks for the great ride," she whispered. "With a little luck and skill, tomorrow we'll ride all the way to the championship." Rapunzel gave the mare a final pat and headed outside. She couldn't wait to see her friends and talk about the joust. It had felt great having them there to cheer her on. She also wanted to get to the Princess School stables so she could take off the heavy armor. Her shoulders and arms ached from holding that lance steady on her charges.

Rapunzel balanced her lance on her shoulder and clanked her way across the field, trying to blend in with the Charm boys. But as one of the few remaining competitors, she was beginning to stand out whether she liked it or not.

"There's Number 17," she heard someone say.

"Did you see his latest move? I've never seen such an agile jouster!" a prince replied. "Hey, do you know who he is?"

Rapunzel grinned beneath her visor. Her techniques were getting the attention she deserved, and so was she! She looked toward the bleachers in search of her friends, but they were nowhere to be seen.

They're probably waiting for me in the stables already, she thought as she climbed over the low hedge on the edge of the Princess School grounds. She hurried to the stable door and yanked it open.

"Your champion has arrived!" she called as she pulled off her helmet. She could hear voices coming from their regular stall, but her friends didn't seem to have heard her.

"Hello?" she called again. She peeked into the stall and saw Ella, Snow, and Rose in a loose huddle.

"Did you see me unseat that last Charmer?" Rapunzel asked, wielding her lance. "You know it was Emmett Pantaloon, right? You know all I need is two more wins and I'll be riding for the title, right?"

"Of course!" Rose replied. "You were great." She hurried over and gave Rapunzel a quick hug, then began to unbuckle and unfasten Rapunzel's armor. "We have to get you out of this thing so we can get to the dwarves' cottage. Snow has some things to show us!"

Rapunzel felt a little disappointed that her friends

85

weren't more excited about her victories. But when she saw Snow's tear-streaked face, her disappointment melted into worry.

"Snow!" she cried as she kicked off her leg armor. "What's the matter?"

Rose pulled the chest plate off of Rapunzel. "We'll explain on the way," she said. "Right now we've got to get going."

The girls hid Rapunzel's armor behind several bales of hay. Then Rapunzel quickly donned her gown and the foursome headed down the forest path that led to Snow's house.

"Snow has been having strange dreams," Ella explained as the girls hurried along. "And then, when she wakes up, they've come true!"

Rapunzel wrinkled her nose in confusion. "What do you mean, they've come true?" she asked.

Snow sniffled. "I know, it sounds crazy. But it's the truth! I'm terrified of what I'll dream next!"

"Show her the golden egg," Ella suggested.

Snow shook her head. "I can show her several," she said. "We're here."

Snow steeled herself and headed across the neatly clipped lawn to the henhouse. Inside, half a dozen hens sat on their nests.

"They all look perfectly normal," Rose murmured as she gazed at the hens.

"You shouldn't judge a book by its cover," Snow said. She reached beneath the tan and speckled bird and retrieved a golden egg, then another, and another.

Rapunzel gasped. "Are they real?"

Snow nodded and handed one of the eggs to her friend. It was warm and heavy.

"I gave one to the dwarves," Snow explained. "I didn't tell them where I got it." She picked up the hen and began to stroke her soft feathers. "They could tell right away that it's real. Then, just to be sure, Mort looked at it wearing his special magnifying glasses — the ones he uses in the mines. That confirmed it. The egg was solid gold."

Rapunzel held an egg up to the sunlight, which glinted off the shimmery surface. "They must be worth ten gold pieces each!"

"Fifteen, according to Gruff," Snow said. "But to me they're not worth a thing. They'll never hatch!"

Ella reached out a comforting hand to Snow just as lovely music echoed in the air.

Snow sighed. "There it is," she said. "It sounds exactly like the harp in my dreams."

Rapunzel led the way out of the henhouse toward the music. It was coming from the grass-roofed garden shed. She opened the door. Next to Snow's garden tools was a harp . . . and it was strumming itself!

"You dreamed this?" Rose asked, pointing to the harp.

"I think so," Snow sobbed. She began to stroke the hen again, this time more frantically. "And if everything I dream keeps coming true . . ." she trailed off, too upset to continue.

"This is very strange," Rapunzel agreed. "How long has it been going on?"

"The climbing dreams have been happening for a week. Then I found the hen and the harp two days ago," Snow said.

Rapunzel cocked her head. "Why didn't you spill the beans sooner?" she asked.

Snow blanched. "The beans!" she cried, nearly dropping the hen. "That's when it started!" She hurried around to the back of the cottage, her friends close behind.

"What was when it start —"

Rose stopped short when she crashed right into Snow's back. Behind her Rapunzel and Ella came to a halt, as well. There, standing right in Snow's backyard, was a beanstalk both taller and thicker than the tallest tree in the forest.

"It's almost as wide as my tower!" Rapunzel cried.

"And as tall as the Princess School towers!" Ella added. "Or taller." The top of it disappeared into the clouds.

Rapunzel walked up to the huge stalk and peered

at it carefully. It was actually three separate stalks that had grown together like a really, *really* thick rope. Bean leaves the size of parasols grew off of the stalk, fluttering in the wind. And all up and down the stalk Rapunzel could make out delicate footprints. It looked as though someone had been climbing the beanstalk!

"Snow, let me see your slippers," Rapunzel said.

Snow lifted the hem of her gown and the girls peered at her shoes. They were flecked with dirt and green stains. "Snow," Rapunzel announced. "You've been climbing this beanstalk in your sleep!"

This time Snow did drop the hen, who squawked loudly. "That can't be!" she cried. But a moment later her big dark eyes widened. "Oh my goodness. It's true! I've been climbing the beanstalk every night!"

Snow looked up the stalk and shuddered. Everything came back to her in a rush. Her dreams hadn't *come* true — they *were* true! "I climb and climb and climb," she whispered. "Up past the clouds. There's a whole kingdom up there, and it's ruled by an awful giant! He lives in a huge stone castle. And he was torturing the poor hen!" The last words came out as a cry.

She reached down and gathered the chicken in her arms. "He was making her lay eggs on command, over and over again, without any rest. And the harp! He made it play awful music. The poor instrument was miserable. I had to save them!"

Rapunzel, Ella, and Rose stared at Snow. Then, all of a sudden, Snow crumpled to the ground in a heap, taking the hen with her. "What am I going to do?" she sobbed.

Chapter Fifteen

Good as Gold

"Let's all go inside," Rose suggested, helping Snow to her feet. "We can have some tea."

Ella picked up the hen, who had been so startled by the fall that she'd laid another golden egg. Ella handed the egg to Rose, then smoothed the chicken's ruffled feathers.

"I could use some applesauce," Snow said with a sniff.

"How about pie?" Rose asked, shooting Ella and Rapunzel a look. The last time they found Snow eating applesauce, her pale skin had been blotchy for days! "You know what too much sauce does to your fair skin." Rose and Rapunzel gently led Snow around the tiny cottage and through the front door. Ella and the magic hen were not far behind.

Inside, Rapunzel got Snow settled at the long table the dwarves had carved from a fallen tree. Then she took out four colorful mugs while Rose put the water on to boil.

Ella set the hen on the floor and sliced up one of Snow's homemade blueberry pies. "This looks delicious, Snow," Ella said.

"The water is ready." Rose filled the teapot and set it down. Soon the girls were gathered around the table with steaming mugs of tea and scrumptious pie.

"I say we take action," Rapunzel said, setting her mug down firmly. "That nasty giant deserves his comeuppance, and the sooner he gets it, the better."

"You've got enough facing off on your plate at the moment, Miss Knight," Rose said, shaking her head. "Besides, if Snow's description is accurate, this giant isn't a creature we want to anger."

"Oh, he's awful!" Snow said, visibly quaking. She rolled a blueberry back and forth across her plate. Then her jaw dropped, as if she'd just thought of something. "What if the dwarves want to go after him? They're only as big as his baby toe!" Snow looked around the cozy cottage. "Why, he could crush this entire cottage with one step!" She shuddered again. "What if he finds out I stole the hen and the harp and does exactly that?" she wailed.

"He won't," Ella said reassuringly. But the look on her face told Rose that she sounded more certain than she felt.

Rapunzel got to her feet and began to pace. "Perhaps

we should cut the beanstalk down," she said, picking up the tiny axe sitting by the fireplace. "He can't descend from his cloud castle if there's no way down, right?"

"I guess not." Snow sniffed. She gazed out the window at the giant stalk. "But I'm still not sure what to do with the hen, the eggs, and the harp. I just can't believe I stole them!" she whimpered.

"You mean *saved* them," Rose consoled her. "You would never have taken them if they were being treated fairly."

"Or if the giant was a good creature," Ella added.

Rapunzel laughed. "Even in your sleep you're a friend to all living things, Snow," she said.

Snow smiled, and Rose sensed that she was feeling a little bit better.

"I have an idea!" Ella suddenly said. "Why don't you give the harp, hen, and eggs to the boy you traded with in the first place? After all, they were his beans to begin with."

Snow clapped her hands together. "That's just what I'll do!" she cried, leaping to her feet. "I'll give them to Jack." She hugged Ella, Rose, and Rapunzel. "Oh, what would I do without friends like you?"

Rose could tell by Snow's lively step that she was feeling much better. She bent easily to pick up the hen, and practically skipped across the yard to the garden shed. "Come with us, magic harp," she chirped. "And we shall deliver you to your new owner!"

Snow handed the harp to Rose and led the way down the path. "I'm not exactly sure where he lives, but I think it's somewhere near the troll bridge," she explained.

Rose nearly panted trying to keep up with Snow. The girl was moving quickly! And she was right about the location of Jack's house, too. Jack was sitting on the front stoop of a small cottage just before the bridge. His chin rested in his hands and he looked glum.

"Hello, Jack," Snow chirped.

Jack looked up at Snow with a confused look on his face, as if he couldn't remember exactly who she was.

"You traded me three beans for a sack of apples, remember?" Snow offered.

Jack suddenly looked nervous. "I hope you're not here for your apples," he whined. "We've eaten the whole bag."

Snow smiled. "No, no," she said cheerfully. "I've brought you a few things."

Jack blinked and scratched his head. But when Snow presented him with the harp, eggs, and hen, he began to rub his hands together greedily.

"Why, these eggs are gold!" he said in disbelief as Snow piled them into his hands.

"It's true," Snow said sadly. "They will never hatch

into adorable chicks." She gazed into the eyes of the speckled hen. "And so this poor hen will never get to be a mother."

"Mother!" Jack exclaimed. "I must show these things to Mother! She will be so pleased with me!" He shoved the eggs into his pockets, tucked the hen under his arm, and grabbed the harp from Ella. Then he turned to go into his house. "See you later!" he called over his shoulder as he shoved the door open with his hip.

"Mother, look what I've brought us!" he shouted. "The hen is magic. She lays golden eggs! Mother, we're rich!"

"What an ungrateful lad!" Ella exclaimed as Jack rambled on about his newfound good fortune. "Why, the boy didn't mention Snow at all!"

"Never mind," Snow said contentedly. "I am just happy to be rid of those reminders of my strange and scary escapades."

Rose put an arm around Snow. "You're as good as gold yourself, Snow," she said warmly.

Rapunzel nodded in agreement. "Only worth so much more."

"Priceless, really," Ella added with a smile.

Snow hugged her friends. "The three of you are what's priceless," Snow said. "I just don't know what I'd do without you! But there is one more reminder we need to get rid of."

Linking arms, the girls made their way back to the dwarves' cottage. They found Mort, Wheezer, Hap, Gruff, Meek, and Dim out back at the base of the beanstalk. Nod was snoozing under a giant bean leaf at the base.

"Look what's been growing in our backyard," Hap called out, holding his cap and scratching his head.

"I know. I'm so sorry!" Snow said fretfully. "It's from the magic beans I planted, and it leads up to a giant's castle!"

"A giant!" Gruff said, waddling across the lawn to join the four girls. The dwarves looked alarmed — except for Gruff, who just looked annoyed.

"We need to chop it down," Rapunzel said flatly.

Mort stroked his beard carefully. "I believe I have just the thing for the job," Mort said, trotting over to the garden shed.

A minute later, Mort was back with a two-handled saw. Six of the dwarves grabbed ahold of one handle. Snow, Ella, Rose, and Rapunzel grabbed the other.

Gruff nudged Nod with his boot, but the sleeping dwarf didn't move. So Mort and Rapunzel carried him out of danger and laid him at the base of a nearby tree. A moment later they began to saw down the beanstalk.

"Heave, ho, ho, heave," they sang. "Chop that stalk and all its leaves!"

Push, pull. Push, pull. Back and forth went twenty arms and the blade of the saw. Finally the beanstalk fell to the ground with an earthshaking thud.

Nod sat up, blinked, and yawned. "Did I miss something?" he asked.

Snow beamed. "Just a little beanstalking," she replied.

Chapter Sixteen

Facing Off

Rapunzel patted Righteous' flanks as she watched the activity on the field. She was on deck, waiting to compete in the next joust. It was hard to believe that the final day of competition had arrived. She'd been waiting for this day for what seemed like forever. But now that it was here she was surprised by her reaction. She thought she'd be filled with excitement and anticipation. What she felt was more like dread.

She could not shake the fear that Val might not forgive her for beating him in front of his schoolmates and family — in front of everyone.

She had felt so funny about it that she had been avoiding walking to and from school with Val since the jousting began — and with no explanation. Each morning he came to collect her as usual, and each morning she hid in her tower until he gave up and then sprinted to school on her own. It was lucky Val hated heights. He would never climb up to check on her. Then in the afternoon Rapunzel hurried to the library where she could look out the diamond-paned window at the drawbridge below, where they usually met. It made her sad to see Val there, waiting patiently, checking the sundial in that garden and finally heading for home.

He just wants to brag, Rapunzel consoled herself. *I'm only teaching him a much needed lesson. He'll understand. Won't he?* The doubt nagged at her.

I've envisioned this as the greatest day of my life, she told herself as Righteous whinnied softly. *What if it becomes one of my worst?*

Rapunzel was so lost in thought she didn't hear the trumpet sound, signaling that the day's competition was about to begin. A rider next to her nudged her gently with his lance.

"You need to prepare to ride," he whispered hoarsely.

Rapunzel started. She'd recognize that voice anywhere. The rider was Val!

"Of course, of course," Rapunzel replied in her deepest voice. Just then a squire took Righteous' reigns and led Rapunzel to their starting point.

Rapunzel readied her lance just as the starting flag was dropped. In a flash Righteous was tearing down the field toward their opponent.

Rapunzel barely had a second to formulate her plan.

The rider charging toward her was tall and looked comfortable in his saddle, but was leaning back slightly. Tipping him off the rear of his horse could be accomplished if she managed to hit him in just the right —

Crash! Rapunzel's lance struck the knight high on his chestplate, and he was thrown straight over the horse's rear to the ground. For a brief moment the rider flailed in the mud before getting to his feet. Then, hanging his head, he led his horse off the field.

Rapunzel rode her mount slowly to the end of the field. "Nice galloping, as usual," Rapunzel told the mare as she patted a sweaty flank. "You are indeed a righteous steed."

With very few riders left in the competition, there was not much time between jousts. By the time Rapunzel was at the end of the field it was nearly time to ride again. This time she tried to push all thoughts of Val out of her mind. When the flag dropped, her lance was ready, but her mind was not clear. Fleeting thoughts of her last opponent looking up at her from the muddy field flickered in her mind.

Without any prompting, Righteous galloped full speed down the field. Rapunzel forced herself to see only what was in front of her, but was bothered by the wind in her ears. Had she just heard her friends call her name?

Righteous and the other horse came together fiercely,

and Rapunzel felt a hard thump in the middle of her chest. One of her feet came out of her stirrup and she struggled to stay in the saddle. Turning Righteous to the left, she swung around just in time to see her opponent's lance coming at her a second time. Instinct overtook and she ducked, thrusting the butt of her own lance at the rider's hip. A moment later he fell to the ground.

Rapunzel's heart hammered in her chest. She had almost been unseated!

You have to focus! she scolded herself. *You won't be getting any second chances!*

Trying to pull herself together, Rapunzel once again rode Righteous to the end of the field. She realized with a start that this was it. She had made it to the final round. There were only two competitors remaining. Only one joust. The moment she had been waiting for had finally arrived. It was just as she had predicted. Rapunzel versus Val. And Rapunzel felt . . .

Sick. This moment was somehow so much bigger — and more important — than she'd ever thought possible. Her head spinning, she fought the urge to rip off her helmet and breathe in gulps of fresh air. She turned her back to the field to clear her head.

You've been training for this moment, she told herself. *And now you must finish what you've started.*

Sitting up straight in her saddle, Rapunzel turned

to face her final opponent. When she saw Val's familiar frame in his own saddle, she longed to pull off her helmet and give him a huge grin and friendly wave, to turn this tournament into one of their fun practices, back to Val and Rapunzel playing like they always did. She could let him win, keep her identity a secret. Just ride away and he would never know. But another part of her wanted something completely different — the chance to prove herself for once and for all. And keeping her secret for a few more minutes was the only way for that to be possible.

"Easy there, Righteous," Rapunzel patted the steed's neck to reassure her. She straightened again in her saddle. All she could do was ride her best.

The flag was tossed and the two horses raced toward each other with remarkable speed. Rapunzel locked her eyes on Val and stared straight ahead as they closed in on each other. Val hunched forward slightly, and certainly didn't seem to be planning on taking it easy on her. She guessed he was going to strike high, and left, just like she taught him. Surely he had no idea who he was facing. A split second before they collided, Rapunzel twisted her body to the side and jabbed Val — hard — on the far side of his shield with her lance. She heard him gasp in surprise as he fell from his horse. The noise from the bleachers was deafening.

As Val got to his feet, he bowed without any hint of disappointment or humiliation.

"I yield to the victor!" he announced to the screaming crowd.

Rapunzel was at once suspicious. Was Val just being a gracious runner-up? That kind of princely behavior was certainly in character. Or had he known all along it was Rapunzel . . . and thrown the joust because he was facing a girl?

Chapter Seventeen

Thrill and Agony

The crowd cheered wildly, and trumpets blared. Rapunzel looked down at Val, her heart hammering in her chest. Did he know it was her? And if not, was he going to be furious when he found out?

Several velvet-clad squires hurried across the field. Four carried a small, carved wooden platform. Two more hefted a rolled-up red carpet. And three more toted a purple and gold portable awning, decorated with fluttering silk streamers. In mere seconds they created a small stage fit for a prince — or princess.

No sooner was the red carpet unrolled than a Charm School official wearing a velvet cape and gold-buckle shoes stepped onto it. Two of the squires, both clad in gold, kneeled before Rapunzel with their arms extended.

Rapunzel's heart soared in sudden realization —

she had won the tournament! She forgot about Val momentarily, swung her leg over Righteous' back, and leaped gracefully to the ground. She looked down at the squires and up at the crowd in the bleachers. All of the Charm School students, Princess School students, and their faculties were on their feet cheering. The Bloomers were loudest of all, and three special princesses were waving and hugging in a most undignified manner. Rapunzel knew Rose, Ella, and Snow were as happy as she. She was about to curtsy to her adoring public when she realized that she was a knight. So she bowed deeply instead.

Then, before she could straighten, the squires reached out to pull her helmet off her head. Part of her wanted to stop them — what if everyone was furious with her? What if she got kicked out of school? But she knew her identity had to be revealed, so she did nothing as they tugged the helmet off, revealing her impossibly large, red-brown coil of hair.

The trumpeters ceased their fanfare. The cheering came to a halt. The field was utterly silent except for the Charm School official in gold-buckle shoes, who sputtered unintelligibly.

Rapunzel looked up at the bleachers. The Charm School boys stared, openmouthed, at their champion. Madame Garabaldi looked like she was about to explode. Lady Bathilde shifted uncomfortably in her seat. Even Rose, Snow, and Ella stopped hugging and looked a bit concerned.

Beside her, Val removed his own helmet and stared at his opponent. "Rapunzel?" he whispered hoarsely.

Rapunzel smiled weakly. "Val, I can explain. I —"

All at once the silence gave way to thunderous cheers. The Bloomers were screaming in a most unregal manner. They threw flowers onto the field and stomped their slippered feet. Soon the Charm School boys joined in, hollering and stomping as well, clearly pleased, if completely surprised, by this shocking upset.

Rapunzel searched Val's face for an outward sign of what he was feeling, but it revealed nothing. She saw him look toward his family, then his friends, in the stands.

"Somebody needed to beat the Charmings," Val murmured. "I only thought it would be me." He shot Rapunzel a meaningful look, then broke into a wide grin. "Excellent riding and lance work, I must admit," he said. "And a few new moves, too!"

Rapunzel felt relief wash through her. Val wasn't angry! And his surprise was genuine — he hadn't known it was she. Suddenly the taste of victory was utterly sweet, with not even a hint of bitterness.

The official in the buckle shoes pulled himself together and cleared his throat. "Access to the famous

Farthingdale Stables goes to . . ." He paused. "Your name, miss?" he asked.

"Rapunzel Arugula of the Princess School Bloomer class," she told him proudly.

"Goes to Rapunzel Arugula and the Princess School Bloomer class," he said, sounding very doubtful. He reached hesitantly for the golden key that hung on a purple ribbon around his neck. But instead of lifting it over his head, he fingered it, reluctant to let it go. Rapunzel wondered if she would indeed be able to claim her prize.

Just then Lady Bathilde appeared next to them. "Sir Salisbury Tims," she said smoothly.

Sir Salisbury let the key drop from his hand and stepped forward. "Eugenia, this is most unusual," he said. "An outrage."

Rapunzel repressed an urge to stomp her foot. Outrage, indeed. She had won fair and square!

Lady Bathilde glanced briefly at Rapunzel. "Let me assure you, Sals, that this was in no way sanctioned by Princess School or its administration. Of course we are terribly grateful for your understanding and generosity. Indeed, it is truly gracious of you to allow Princess School to take part in your illustrious tournament. Should we wish to enter a Princess School champion in the future, we will of course request permission beforehand."

Rapunzel looked at her feet humbly. Though she detected a glimmer of pride in her headmistress' voice, she felt badly for putting her in this position. Fortunately, Lady Bathilde was respected by virtually the entire kingdom. If anyone could smooth ruffled feathers, it was she.

"Of course, of course," Sir Salisbury replied. "As you know, gallantry is our highest priority here at Charm," he added with a smile. He reached once again for the key to the stables, this time removing it easily and placing it over Rapunzel's head.

Once more the crowd erupted, and trumpets blasted. Rapunzel turned to the bleachers and curtsied. Flowers dotted the field, and Rapunzel bent to pick one up. When she straightened, her classmates and friends surrounded her, engulfing her in a giant hug.

"You did it!" Ella exclaimed, jumping up and down.

Rose pulled off a gauntlet and squeezed her hand. "I knew you would win!" she cried.

"Not without all of you," Rapunzel admitted. She looked at Ella, Rose, and Snow in turn. "How are you today, Snow?" she asked.

"Perfect!" Snow replied with a beaming smile. "I slept like a baby all night, and had a wonderful dream about my father. And now I'll get to meet all those beauties in the Farthingdale Stables, too!"

"Hey, make room for the second-place finisher," Val said, gently elbowing his way toward Rapunzel.

"Oh, Val!" Rapunzel said, throwing her arms around him. "You're the greatest sport I know. And I'm so sorry I wasn't there to walk to and from school with you," she added quietly. "It was just so hard — and strange — to keep a secret from you."

"A secret?" Val replied, feigning surprise. "I knew it was you all along, of course."

Behind him, Dap appeared, shaking his head vehemently. "No, you didn't," he insisted. "You wouldn't have been so sure of yourself if you had!"

Val's cheeks turned as pink as Rose's gown. "Well . . ." he said slowly. "Maybe I wasn't *sure* it was you. But I had my suspicions."

Rapunzel smiled and thumped her oldest friend on the back. "Well, I definitely knew it was my pal Val all along," she said. "That's why I took it easy on you!"

About the Authors

Jane B. Mason grew up in Duluth, Minnesota, where a round stone tower graces the top of the city's hillside. (Fortunately, she was never trapped inside.) She had a strict mother and three older sisters who made her do her share of chores but never tried to keep her home from a school dance.

Sarah Hines Stephens grew up in Twain Harte, California, where she caught frogs in the woods but rarely kissed them. She can't talk to birds and she is hardly royalty, but her name does mean "princess," and after dating a toad or two, she married a real prince of a guy.

Currently, Sarah and Jane lead charmed lives in Oakland, California. They are great friends and love to write together. Some of their other books include *The Little Mermaid and Other Stories, Heidi, Paul Bunyan and Other Tall Tales, The Legend of Sleepy Hollow, The Nutcracker, The Jungle Book,* and *King Arthur*, all Scholastic Junior Classics, and *The Best Christmas*. Between them, Sarah and Jane have two husbands, five kids, three dogs, one cat, and a tomato worm named Bob.

Look for the next book in The Princess School series:

Apple-y Ever After

Here's a sneak peek!

Chapter One
Bluebird

"Mmm . . . hmmmm." Snow White's cheery hum turned into a long sigh as she sat down on the cushion of her chair in the hearthroom chamber of Princess School. The simple song she had been thinking of was not making her smile as it usually did. In fact, smiling felt like a great effort.

Snow's lips arced up automatically toward her pink cheeks when she saw her friends Briar Rose, Cinderella Brown, and Rapunzel Arugula come through the classroom door. They all smiled aaved at her, but the moment they took their seats, Snow's mouth drooped and she sighed again, more loudly. Feeling blue took a lot out of her.

Ducking behind the piled-up hairdo of the princess in front of her, Snow propped her heavy head on her hands while Madame Garabaldi, the First-year Bloomers' hearthroom teacher, rapped out scroll call. It just wasn't like Snow to feel down, especially here at Princess School. She loved learning how to be a proper princess, especially with Ella, Rapunzel, and Rose in her class. Normally, Snow woke up smiling and excited to skip off to school. But that morning, she had woken up uneasy. She wasn't sure what could be the matter or how to make herself feel glad again.

Snow gazed through the tall, diamond-paned window, hoping to spot a happy distraction. Usually a simple glimpse of a flitting bird or a squirrel on a branch would make Snow giggle and clap her hands with delight. But not this morning.

With her chin in her palm, Snow counted at least three bluebirds winging outside without cracking a smile. Even as the birds came closer and closer, swooping and flapping, Snow remained glum.

She watched the birds land on the window ledge and bob their tiny heads as if they were trying to look through the glass.

"Snow White!" Madame Garabaldi called loudly.

"Yes?" Snow White sat up straight. She had been so busy watching the birds she forgot about scroll call. "I mean, present . . . Madame," she added.

"I'm quite pleased to hear it," Madame Garabaldi said evenly. "For a moment I felt certain you were somewhere else." Her steely gaze rested on the top of Snow's carved wooden desk. "Elbows off," she said crisply.

Snow blushed and put her hands in her lap. She had to be especially careful around Madame Garabaldi so as not to let the hearthroom teacher see the bad habits Snow had picked up from the dwarves. Mort, Meek, Hap, Nod, Wheezer, Dim, and Gruff were loads of fun and loved Snow dearly, but they were not very regal-mannered.

As soon as the instructor lowered her eyes to the scroll-call parchment, Snow turned back to the window. The bluebirds were still there, looking in more intently than ever. One of them tapped lightly on the glass, and a moment later the other two joined in.

They sound as if they're knocking to be admitted! Snow thought, managing a small grin. She could not shake the feeling that they were looking at her. And she wasn't the only one who noticed.

Ella turned and leaned across the aisle. "Snow, I think those birds are trying to tell you something!" she said in a hushed whisper.

"Oh, I'm sure they aren't here for me," Snow whispered back. She had befriended each and every bird throughout the land, but what would they want with her while she was in class?

THUNK!

All of the girls in the chamber jumped as a large tern landed heavily on the sill, spotted Snow White, and joined in tapping on the glass.

Snow's brow furrowed uncharacteristically. She had to admit that the birds were most certainly focused on her. So was Madame Garabaldi, and she clearly was not amused by the rapping and flapping fowl. Snow felt her pale face redden again as the stern teacher looked from her to the growing aviary outside.

Flustered, Snow motioned the birds away with her hand. But they kept pecking, louder and louder. When the instructor's back was turned, Snow quickly stood and made flapping gestures with her pale arms.

"Fly away," she whispered desperately. "Fly away!"

A few of the other Bloomers in class giggled, but Snow's friends looked befuddled and concerned. And the birds . . . well, either they could not understand or they did not want to.

At the front of the chamber, Madame Garabaldi read a long list of announcements from an ivory scroll. Snow wasn't able to concentrate on a single one. *Tap . . . tap . . . tappity . . . tap-tappity.* The pecking continued like a strange percussion performance. More and more birds arrived. Soon seagulls were circling and screeching loudly with their laughterlike call. Robins, budgies, and other small birds chimed in with more delicate tweets. Crows cawed and owls screeched. And all of them took turns pecking at the window. It was like a symphony gone awry.

"Snow, can't you do something?" Rose whispered from the next aisle.

Several Bloomers were staring open-mouthed at the mass of birds on the windowsill. And none of them was even pretending to listen to their teacher.

"Maybe we should let them in," Rapunzel said with a mischievous grin.

Finally Madame Garabaldi grabbed the golden tassel holding back the heavy velvet drapes. With a flick of her wrist, she let the tassel fall free, and the heavy curtains swung over the glass. Snow caught a glimpse of several huge pelicans gliding in for a landing before the birds disappeared behind the velvet.

The light in the room grew dim and the noise of the birds became a bit more muffled. "Grimm nonsense." Madame Garabaldi frowned.

"Yes, Grimm," Snow repeated softly. It was certainly possible that the witches who attended the nearby Grimm School were stirring up potions that would make the birds act strangely. Still, Snow was not convinced. It really seemed that the birds were trying to communicate something to her . . . something important.

Madame Garabaldi clapped her hands rapidly and

a page stepped forward from the back of the room. He looked a bit guilty as he tried to hide a yawn and straighten his pointy hat.

"This is an awful nuisance!" Madame Garabaldi stated as she wrote something on a small scroll. "Lady Bathilde must be informed of this disturbance at once."

Taking the scroll, the page bowed several times and backed out of the chamber. Snow did not envy his task of bringing bad news to the headmistress.

When the trumpet sounded to mark the end of class, the princesses filed delicately into the marble halls, whispering behind gloved hands about the birds' strange behavior. Snow found herself surrounded by her own flock of non-feathered friends. They padded together over the polished pink-and-white tile floor.

"What do you know, Snow?" Rapunzel asked in her usual frank manner.

"Nothing." Snow said, biting her lower lip to keep from crying. She was feeling terribly nervous.

"Can you think of any reason those birds would be here to see you?" Rose asked gently.

Ella, Rapunzel, and Rose all looked at Snow expectantly. She could tell they had noticed she felt shaken.

Snow opened her mouth to answer Rose, but before anything came out there was a clatter of claws and beaks on the window beside them.

"Goodness!" Snow exclaimed, alarmed. She turned toward the birds. "Shoo!" Snow said sweetly to the seagulls clamoring at the glass. "*Please* shoo!" she begged. Out of the corner of her eye Snow saw Lady Bathilde hurrying down the corridor with an unusual scowl on her face.

"I'll have to have the groundskeeper purchase extra cleaning supplies," Snow heard the elegant headmistress declare. "The excess excrement must not stain the castle!"

Snow heard Rapunzel's stifled laugh and turned back toward the window. The gulls were gazing through the glass at her with such imploring looks that it was undeniably clear. The birds were here for her. But what did they want, and how could she prevent them (and herself) from getting into trouble?

Ella. Snow. Rapunzel. Rose
Four friends who wait for no prin

Ella's first day of Princess
School is off to a lousy start.
Then she meets Snow, Rapun
and Rose. Ella's new friends
make Princess School fun—bu
can they help her stand up to
her horrible steps in time for
Coronation Ball?

The Princess School: If the Shoe Fits
by Jane B. Mason and Sarah Hines Steph
0-439-54532-3 • $4.99

The Maiden Games are fast
approaching and Snow Whit
is frozen with fear. She'll be
facing off against the nasty
witches from the Grimm
School. Even worse, her awfu
stepmother is one of the judge

The Princess School: Who's the Fairest
by Jane B. Mason and Sarah Hines Stephen
0-439-56553-7 • $4.99

Available wherever you buy books.